ALOHA HIDEAWAY INN

GETAWAY BAY RESORT ROMANCE, BOOK 1

ELANA JOHNSON

ONE

STACEY STAPLETON REPLACED the phone in its fancy-pants cradle, casting it a glare as if it had done her a personal wrong. Everything about this room on the fifteenth floor screamed high-end, and there was no way for her to replicate it. Number one, she only had one floor, so she could never provide the bay view that this new hotel, Sweet Breeze, did.

Number two, she was currently saving every penny she had to replace the carpet in the five rooms she had available at her bed and breakfast, and she now had a huge charge sitting on her credit card for this little espionage escapade she'd indulged herself in.

She should've known coming to Sweet Breeze was a bad idea. The air here felt a little too sticky, the smiles on the staff's faces a little too sweet, and the service a little too slick.

"I don't need to replicate it," she said. People didn't come to Getaway Bay for the high-tech room phones or even the five-hundred thread count sheets on the king bed where she sat to wait for her room service order.

"Shoot." She dove for her phone, which she'd left on the clear glass top of the dresser. She started the timer on her phone, mentally telling herself to add a minute to the delivery time. No way this place could provide her a breakfast in the amount of time her cooks could down the beach at Aloha Hideaway.

Plus, while the view was nice for the first selfie or two, Stacey herself much preferred the privacy her bed and breakfast provided, the way the jungle grew right up to the building, almost like it was trying to erase the evidence of mankind's existence on the island, and the sound of waves from the nearby beach.

Here, she couldn't even open the window. The best she could do was press a button set into the wall near the bed to simulate the wave sounds. Lame.

With her timer going, and her stay coming to an end, Stacey gathered her personal hygiene items and got in the shower. The spray was hot and strong and perfectly fantastic. So this ritzy hotel that had been siphoning off customers for the ten months since it had opened had excellent showers.

Did people really choose a place to stay based on a shower review?

"Nope," she said into the spray. Then she turned and squirted some of the hibiscus-scented body wash out of the dispenser stuck to the wall. "And they're going to waste a ton of money with this thing." Just to prove her point, she sent a few squirts of the surely expensive soap directly onto the floor of the tub.

She scrubbed herself down, wondering why the owner of Sweet Breeze couldn't just provide those tiny bottles of bland body wash like every other hotel in the area. Her frustration frothed like the luxury bubbles still foaming on her loofa, and she turned to wash off, wishing her negative attitude and desperation would go down the drain too.

She slipped on the excess body wash she'd deliberately wasted, her arms splaying to the sides, searching for something to grab onto. But this shower was impossibly smooth on all sides, and she ended up grabbing onto the shower curtain. It wasn't even standard, as it didn't rip off the rod like hers would have.

Cursing herself for being spiteful, she found her feet and regained her balance, smoothing down the shower curtain like it was a cat. She almost expected it to start purring, not that she had any experience with a content cat.

Her feline friend was as grumpy as they came, and Malificent skulked around the bed and breakfast with a general disdain that applied to everything she came in contact with. If Stacey even tried to pet her, she was met with a hiss and the baring of claws. So she put out food and water and let the cat do what it wanted. No sense in poking the bear. Or in this case, the tabby.

She got out of the shower and dried off, pulling her reddish hair into a turban with a second towel. Heaven knew this place could afford to launder an extra towel, and she considered throwing a perfectly clean one on the floor too.

In the end, she remembered the fiasco with the body wash and left the unused towels on the rack. Plus, she wanted to do her part to use water wisely and a pin of guilt pushed into her heart that she'd used two towels when she could've done the job with one.

Back in the room, her phone had just ticked past the twelve-minute mark. "Seriously, how long does it take to make French toast?" she asked the spacious room. She'd booked their basic room, with one king bed, over a month ago, under a different name. She wasn't sure why. The owner of this swanky new monstrosity on Getaway Bay lived across the Pacific, probably in his equally ridiculous penthouse overlooking the city of Los Angeles.

No one from the Davenport Development Group would ever know who she was or when she'd stayed with them. They had supervisors and managers and assistants to handle everything for average guests like Jaida Moore, the name she'd registered under.

At Aloha Hideaway, Stacey managed everything. Sure, she had a small staff that were like family to her, but when the buck stopped, it was always in her wing of the house she'd inherited from her grandfather five years ago.

She started to dress, leaving her wet towel pooled at her feet. A loud, hollow noise came from the window, causing her to jolt with shock and fear. Her heart pounded up into her throat, and she hurried over to the pane she couldn't open to find a smudge of...something. A feather drifted down on the other side of the glass, time slowing as it wafted back and forth, back and forth.

A bird had just flown into the hotel. Probably a pigeon,

which in Stacey's opinion, were the rats of the bird world. But still. A living creature had died because of this towering building on the beach that totally did *not* belong. Even Hawaii's fowl knew Sweet Breeze shouldn't be here.

Something clicked behind her, and she spun, her pulse dancing from the front of her ribcage to the back.

"Room service," a deep voice said and a cart started to push open the door.

A squeak of surprise flew from Stacey's mouth and she tried to cover her bra with her bare arms as she half hopped, half tiptoed back around the corner.

"I'm not dressed," she managed to say, her voice trembling and weak, two things Stacey never allowed anyone to see. In front of her family, her staff, her friends in the Women's Beach Club, Stacey was calm, cool, controlled. She cracked jokes and ordered extra fruity drinks for everyone. She gave people weekends off and brought pineapple cookie monster salad to family picnics.

And now she was currently wearing only her bra and panties, and apparently the man pushing the cart through the door hadn't heard her.

"I'm not dressed," she called again, and the squeaky wheels on the cart stopped.

"You ordered room service?"

"Yes, but I need a few minutes to put on some pants." Did this guy speak English? She hadn't seen him in her haste to conceal herself behind the wall, and she bent to grab the first article of clothing she could.

It was her bathing suit cover-up and she pulled it on. Her

bra straps stuck out the top, but at least she was as covered as she would be on the beach.

The door slammed closed, but the edge of the cart remained. Stacey took a deep breath and dared to peek around the corner, finding the man gone and her food producing the delicious aroma of bacon and sweet maple syrup.

"Impossible," she muttered as she looked at her phone. With all the commotion, she decided to subtract the minute she'd been planning to add on and saw her phone said the food had been delivered in thirteen minutes and twenty-four seconds.

"Ridiculous." She wasn't sure if she was talking about herself or the room service. She also wasn't sure if she could produce food as quickly.

She lifted the cloche and found condensation on the inside of it. This food was still hot.

"Unbelievable." Stacey wondered if she'd ever speak in full sentences again. It seemed her whole vocabulary was made of single words. She looked at the cloche in disgust. They were probably ordered from somewhere secret, like the Cloche Underground or something. The metal looked like brushed nickel, far superior to anything Stacey had ever gotten from the restaurant supply store on the other side of the island.

Knocking sounded on the door. "Are you dressed now?"

He probably wanted a tip. And delivering a piping hot, smells-so-good-her-stomach-rumbled breakfast in only thirteen minutes, he deserved one.

Stacey shimmied out of the cover-up and pulled on a

maxi dress in dark purple, the color of the hibiscus flowers that could only be found in the gardens at Aloha Hideaway. Her grandfather had cultivated them, cross-breeding the flowers to produce the unique color, the blooms fringed with white, and then he'd patented it. Now Stacey had three workers who dedicated full-time hours to the gardens, and she made a nice profit from selling them to locals, other hotels, cab companies, travel agents, and anyone who wanted to provide a special Hawaiian experience to the tourists arriving on the big island.

After squeezing past the cart, she pulled open the door, ready to chew the man out for entering her room without knocking first. She opened her mouth as her voice lost its ability to form sound.

The man standing in the hall didn't look like the serving type. He had strong, broad, powerful shoulders that spanned nearly the width of the doorway. His body narrowed to his waist, where he'd tied a long, black apron. He wore a black pair of slacks beneath that, with a black shirt that strained across the chest and biceps.

His blue eyes, almost the same beautiful ocean blue as the bay beyond the window, pierced hers, and went well with his military-style haircut and clean-shaven face. He was tall, tan, and muscular, perfect for a pair of board shorts for early morning surfing, or the board room for an afternoon meeting.

"Sorry about that," he said, and his bass voice caused vibrations to tumble through Stacey's chest. They also got her heart going again, which sent blood to her brain, which told her voice to *say something!*

"It's fine."

Not that!

He rubbed his thumb across his right eyebrow, drawing her attention to the slice through the middle of it, like he'd been in a knife fight and lost. But he was too clean-cut for a knife fight, and Stacey's mind ran rampant with possibilities for that scar on his face.

"How's the food?" He nodded behind her, obviously seeing that she'd removed the cloche while he stood in the hall.

"I haven't actually tried it. But it's hot, so that's good." Why she was speaking at all, she didn't know. This server didn't need her critique of the food. "And delivered fast. Thirteen—I mean, less than fifteen minutes. Wow."

A smile pulled across his strong mouth, rendering Stacey weak in the wrong places and staring at such a gorgeous grin. Men as good-looking as him didn't seem fair. She wondered what his life had been like. Did he get special treatment in school? Did anyone ever tell him no? When he got pulled over for speeding, did he walk away with a ticket the way she did?

"Thank you." She held out a twenty-dollar bill. A ridiculous tip, but probably one that was expected for a hotel-resort such as Sweet Breeze.

He waved the money away without even glancing at it. There was something...not quite right about him. What room service attendant turned down money?

"Sorry about barging in. I thought...." The grin appeared again, and Stacey almost leaned against the wall so he wouldn't see how he affected her. "Sorry."

She nodded since her voice had gone on vacation again, and he turned and walked away. Wow, the view from the back was just as spectacular as the front, and Stacey pulled herself back into the room before he reached the corner just in case he turned back from the weight of her stare.

She leaned against the closed door and pressed one hand over her heart. She felt stupid for a lot of reasons, the biggest one being that she'd felt a spark of attraction for the handsome stranger who'd almost seen her naked.

TWO

FISHER DUPONT practically punched open the black plastic door that led into the kitchens.

Keep it together, he told himself again. He'd been reciting it the whole way down from the fifteenth floor. He'd donned these ill-fitting clothes and practically shaved his head in an attempt to keep his identity hidden from the staff. He wanted to operate on the ground floor of Sweet Breeze, find out how the systems worked—if they were even working—and what the staff thought needed to be improved.

"Do we really just go into rooms with the orders?" he asked the head concierge, Kepa, on room service, only a slight growl to his words.

Kepa, much shorter than Fisher's six-foot-five frame, stared up at him. "Who told you that?"

Fisher pressed his lips together. He didn't want to say, because Kepa likely had the power to fire anyone on his staff. "No one."

"Did you do that? Enter a guest's room without knocking and announcing yourself?"

Fisher considered the man, who's dark eyes felt like coal filled with fire. "Yes."

Kepa's nostrils flared and he held out his hand as if Fisher would put something in it.

"What?" he asked, not connecting the dots. And he'd made a living out of drawing his own dots and connecting them into pictures no one else had imagined before.

"Your apron. You're fired." Kepa wore sympathy in his eyes, but Fisher didn't detect any leeway in his decision.

So he untied the apron he'd only been wearing for an hour and handed it to the room service supervisor.

"What room?" Kepa asked.

"Fifteen-twenty-one." Fisher had an amazing memory with numbers, but he kept some facts about himself close to the vest. This was one such thing.

"I'll send someone to apologize. You should go." He flicked two fingers toward someone behind Fisher. "Please see this man off the premises."

Fisher allowed himself to be led out of the hotel he owned, getting in the car he'd rented down the street and driving away as if he had an island home to go to. In reality, he'd gone to work in his hotel that morning from the penthouse that took up the entire twenty-eighth floor. It swayed when the wind coming off the bay was really bad, but after ten months of living there, Fisher had gotten used to it. Kind of.

He pulled over at a gas station and went inside. "Restroom?"

The guy behind the counter looked him up and down, apparently decided he wasn't going to vandalize the bathroom, and handed Fisher a tiny brass key attached to a two-foot-long piece of piping that had been painted bright purple and had the state flower of Hawaii doodled in black marker all over it.

Fisher would never tire of the beautiful flowers in this island paradise. He'd needed a fresh start after a disastrous business venture with his father, and he'd taken it here in Getaway Bay. He no longer wanted to get away from his own life, so that was a definite improvement.

In the bathroom, he stripped out of the bad clothes and pulled his midnight-colored suit from his small satchel. Properly dressed, he could now return to the hotel, figure out who was staying in room fifteen-twenty-one, and make sure she understood that his staff did not barge into rooms just because they had a room service cart.

He handed the pipe-key back to the clerk. "Thanks." He needed coffee, stat, but he wasn't going to get it from a gas station. He'd had plenty of such brew in the past, and it was never quite up to his taste standard. No, there'd be much better coffee at the hotel, and he decided he could wait.

The man stared at him, and Fisher was sure his suit had cost as much as the clerk made in a year. He used to feel bad about his wealth, but he contributed to so many charities now, and he considered himself a pretty nice guy, so he didn't let the guilt pin him down for long. Plus, he'd worked too hard for too long to have a bleeding heart because he could afford the suits, the leather shoes, the fancy cars, the jets.

After returning the nondescript sedan to the rental company and getting behind the wheel of his convertible, he returned to Sweet Breeze, taking full advantage of the valet.

"Good morning, Mister DuPont," Sterling said as he opened the door. "Nice haircut."

Fisher stood and smiled, the haircut courtesy of Marshall Robison. Marshall could wield a pair of clippers as well as he ran his generational pineapple plantations, but Fisher's best friend and fellow founder of the Hawaii Nine-0 club had gone a little crazy with the blades.

He ran his hand along his nearly bald scalp, hoping his hair would grow back quickly. He'd have to slather sunscreen everywhere up top to make sure he didn't get a nasty burn in spots usually covered by his hair.

"Thanks. Is Owen in?"

"Arrived an hour ago, sir. I believe he said he had business in the gardens this morning." Sterling smiled and saluted before sliding behind the wheel of Fisher's car.

He took an extra moment to pull his jacket closed and button it before he entered his hotel. He walked differently in the suit than he had in the servant clothes, and he made a note of it. Why did it matter what he wore? Was it because every eye swiveled to him when he wore suits like this? Every back straightened? Every employee brightened, smiled, and then got back to work?

Fisher wasn't sure, but he did know he didn't like the attention. He craved the anonymity the room service staff enjoyed, just like he'd basked in being able to walk around his hotel without scrutiny while he pushed a laundry cart in front of him.

That had been an interesting day, as he'd had no idea the enormity of linens, towels, cloth napkins from the four on-site restaurants, and other items the laundry staff took care of. He didn't know his hotel received bonuses for being under a certain limit for water usage, and he'd really learned a lot from the small army of people he employed—and who'd embraced him as one of their fellow laundromatters —in only an eight-hour shift.

Still, when the time was right, he wore the suits and played the part. Mostly because it was better than any of the alternatives he'd tried, and the show gave him something to fill his day with.

He bypassed the front desk and the guest elevators. Holding his thumb against a pad, he opened the lock to his private hallway and let the door snick closed behind him. His elevator would take him to any floor, and he pressed the fifteen, hoping a personal visit from the hotel owner would be enough to convince the curvy woman in room fifteen-twenty-one not to write a damaging review about his wait staff. About *him*.

The elevator spit him out with a ding, and he plucked a pair of thick, black-framed glasses from his breast pocket, sliding them into place on his face. Women claimed that they would've known Superman was Clark Kent, that Lois Lane was *so stupid*, but he found the glasses disguised him as well as a ball cap and the wrong clothes. It was almost like the glasses simply threw people off, and they spent so much time trying to make the three-thousand-dollar suit line up with the cheap, plastic frames that he was gone before they put the pieces together.

Plus, they covered up that slight scar in his eyebrow.

Fisher strode toward the door where he'd delivered breakfast only thirty minutes ago. He knocked this time, when every instinct had told him to last time. He'd have to have a talk with Peni about telling new-hires to enter rooms without knocking. Of course that wasn't how they did things at Sweet Breeze, and Fisher should've known better.

The same woman pulled open the door, her striking green eyes somehow penetrating right past his expensive defenses. Her hair tumbled and curled, falling below her shoulders in the most delicious shade of red he'd ever seen. He had a thing for redheads, though he'd never dated one.

And you're not here to ask for her number.

"Good morning," he said, his voice perfectly professional and crisp. "I understand there was a slight mishap here this morning."

"I already got an apology," she said, her eyes narrowing.

Fisher could practically see the wheels turning in her head. She looked vaguely familiar, though he couldn't place where he would've seen her before. He rarely interacted with the guests, and he'd only just begun making the rounds through his undercover operations to work in all the departments of his hotel. He went around town, but usually to reserved private rooms where he was ushered in and out without making a fuss. Heaven knew the presence of his hotel on this island alone had made enough turbulence for a while.

"Yes, my room service supervisor is fantastic." He put his CEO smile on his face. It had guided him successfully through many board meetings and swayed construction foremen—tough, stubborn men—toward his side of certain issues in critical moments.

"I wanted to come personally assure you that our room service attendants always knock and announce themselves before entering."

"Clearly, not always." She leaned her hip into the doorjamb and kept one handful of fingers curled around the door, barely letting him see inside. The smile on her face could only be described as…satisfied.

"Yes, well, from now on. Can I gift you a free night here at Sweet Breeze for the misunderstanding?" Heck, she could ask for a week and Fisher would give it to her. Something itched along his collar, but he kept his hands pleasantly at his sides. The urge to smooth down the eyebrow that seemed to constantly want to go the wrong direction tugged, pulled, yanked at his resolve. He couldn't do it; he'd done it in front of her as the attendant. Such a gesture was too identifying.

"Yeah," the woman said, a smile that felt flirty stealing across her face and making her twice as beautiful. "I'll take a free night."

Fisher's heart was doing something weird in his chest, but he managed to nod and say, "I'll have my guest concierge have the certificate ready for you when you check out." He extended his hand for her to shake.

The moment she touched him, an earthquake that could've registered on the Richter scale shook his body. Her smile stayed hitched in place, and Fisher added his to the conversation.

"Thank you, Miss…."

"Sta—Moore. Jaida Moore." Her smile turned false, and Fisher hadn't built himself into a billionaire real estate mogul by not being able to detect a lie. He'd worked with enough carpenters, electricians, plumbers, and brick masons to know when corners were being cut. He'd seen everything from upright, honest men doing good work and making a good living to sleazy, sloppy work that tried to get passed off as adequate.

He certainly knew when he was being lied to, and Miss Jaida Moore wasn't very good at it.

"Very well, Miss Moore," he said, keeping his voice smooth, non-emotional. "Stop by the concierge desk before you go to get your certificate."

"Most people call them coupons," she said, her left eyebrow quirking in a way that felt challenging to Fisher. Slightly condescending too.

"Yes, well, Sweet Breeze doesn't offer coupons." He buttoned his jacket and gave an authoritative nod. "Have a great day, Miss Moore."

"You too, Mister Davenport."

Fisher froze as he turned, his muscles turning hard at the name. How had she known it? And why would she use it? His stare lasted long enough for her to bring back the grin, a little cockier and more sure of herself than before.

She lifted one shoulder into a sexy shrug that made Fisher wish he'd met this woman after a morning spent in the surf instead of while he was "Mister Davenport."

"I can Google, you know."

"Ah." He ducked his head, something inside him telling

him to get out of there before the conversation turned too dangerous. "Until next time."

He walked away, glad for the first time that he'd registered the hotel under his father's conglomerate. She didn't need to know that Fisher had given up his slime ball father's name twenty-five years ago, when the man had walked out on him and his mother. She didn't need to know he'd gotten the scar in his eyebrow on one of his father's job sites, because the man cut corners as easily as he breathed. Hardly anyone knew those things, and Fisher was going to keep it that way, even if Jaida-whose-name-wasn't-Jaida stirred something in him he'd thought long dormant.

THREE

STACEY ARRIVED AT ALOHA HIDEAWAY, a sense of peace descending on her that she'd missed during her overnight stay just down the beach. There were several smaller hotels along the main drag that ran the length of Getaway Bay, as well as three bed and breakfasts dotting the area. Hers was tucked away between palm trees and a few acres of wild forest, with so much greenery, flowers, and four water features, the online pictures almost didn't look real.

But they were real, and Stacey had people to maintain all the amenities of her business. She needed to, because there was no way she could refurnish the rooms with luxury beds like the one she'd slept in last night. She didn't have funds for bigger flatscreen TVs. She almost had enough for new carpet, and she could refresh the rooms with paint once the summer season died off.

Breakfast had ended an hour ago, and Stacey's all-female

staff was in full swing as the hour of check-out approached. Then they'd have a few hours of seemingly calm, where they all worked feverishly before check-in began.

Stacey's busiest days were Thursdays and Sundays with people coming to the Bay for the weekend. Sometimes Monday could be hairy too, if she had families staying with her, as they tended to tack on an extra day just to go to the beach.

The beach called to Stacey now, and she knew only the warm sand, bright sunshine, and rhythmic lapping of the waves would truly erase that tall, delicious man from her mind. He needled her thoughts, and not only because he was as handsome and polished as the day was long. There was something...not quite right about him.

If she'd had the opportunity, she'd put the classy, sophisticated Davenport who'd come to apologize in a police line-up—right next to the room service attendant. Perhaps they were brothers, though none of her online digging had produced evidence of more than one Davenport heir.

"How'd breakfast go?" she asked Betty as she stepped into the kitchen. Though Betty came in a short, petite package, she had a whip-like personality with a loud voice to match. Everyone listened to her, Stacey included, because Betty had more experience in the bed and breakfast industry than anyone else on the Aloha Hideaway staff.

She'd attended culinary school on the mainland and opened four restaurants back in Hawaii by the age of thirty. Now fifty-five, her hair had turned completely gray, but her steel-colored eyes had not lost a single ounce of their edge.

"Excellent," she said as she scrubbed steel wool across

ALOHA HIDEAWAY INN   23

the flattop. "All five rooms came to eat. There was plenty. We're set for Kalua pork for dinner tonight."

The scent of sugar and smoke hung in the air as Stacey nodded. Betty arrived at the B&B at five o'clock every morning, hit the ground running, and had breakfast on the table at eight, as promised, seven days a week.

Aloha Hideaway never served lunch, though they would make picnic lunches upon special request. Dinner was served seven nights a week as well, and Betty usually did most of the prep and then left the rest for the night cook, Dillan.

"Mm, I love Thursdays." Stacey flashed Betty a smile as she walked through the kitchen toward the door on the other side. The kitchen was the hub of the sprawling house, with the main living room in front of it. Stacey had converted that into an airy, natural-light lobby by widening the front doors of what used to be a house and introducing more wild plants and a fountain.

Her bed and breakfast might not have all the bells and whistles that Sweet Breeze did, but it offered a lot more. More Hawaiian culture. More attention to detail. More charm. Feeling confident now that she'd stayed in the imposing building down the beach, she reached the door that led to the east wing of the house. Her private wing. Her employee's quarters.

"I've never heard you say you like Thursdays before." Betty shook her head with a smile, her arms still pumping, pumping, pumping to get the flattop clean. The woman worked hard, and the kitchen ran without a speed bump, exactly how Stacey needed it to.

"Well, there's a first time for everything," Stacey said, pulling open the door and stepping through it. A long, cobbled hallway ran down the middle of this wing, the same way it did on the west side. There were five bedrooms over here, and five in the west wing. Stacey had chosen the largest bedroom, which was also the farthest from the center of the house, as her own.

The rooms on this side of the home didn't have their own bathrooms, but she'd renovated the west wing to include that. Guests didn't like sharing a bathroom or coordinating shower schedules with strangers.

Stacey had her own bathroom, and there were two more in this wing. Marge, her architectural landscaper that kept the grounds interesting and beautiful, lived in the bed and breakfast with Stacey. She had her own room and bathroom.

The other two rooms were furnished like guest rooms, but Stacey didn't rent them out. Her staff used them as break rooms, as places of refuge from the service industry that could get tiresome and heavy at times. The third room was used for storage, for little bars of soap, and fresh towels, and the rows and rows of shelves in that room actually soothed Stacey.

Her evening manager slept in the first bedroom for a few hours each night. Her maids took siestas while they waited for guests to check-out and leave rooms to be cleaned.

She heard chatter up ahead and stopped in the doorway to poke her head into the last bedroom on the left. Her four youngest employees, all in their late twenties or early thirties sat around a table, mugs of hot liquid in front of them.

Stacey knew Ashley only drank tea. She worked exclusively in the hibiscus gardens with the girl on her right, Bailey. Lizzie and Tayla were dressed in their maid uniforms, one sipping hot chocolate if the marshmallows were any indication, and the other nursing what looked like black coffee.

"Morning, ladies," Stacey said. Her staff didn't jump to attention the way she'd seen the employees at Sweet Breeze.

"Morning," they all chorused back. Stacey enjoyed the more casual relationship she had with her employees, and she wondered if dark, dangerous Davenport even knew how to be casual. What would that look like on him? Jeans? A T-shirt? Swim trunks? She couldn't imagine the imposing man who'd shown up at her door wearing that expensive suit in anything but crisp, white shirts and pressed designer slacks.

"Anything to report?" Stacey asked.

"Nope," Ashley said while the other girls shook their heads.

"All right. Complete the checklists and let me know our needs." Stacey gave them a smile and continued toward her suite. She put in an order for supplies and food on Thursdays, which also added to the general busyness. But she'd found it to be the best day to do an order, because then she was never short-supplied for her busiest times.

She depended on her support staff to turn in their checklists, so she could order the right items at the right time. But it would be another couple of hours before they'd be slid under her door and her gardeners went outside and her maids moved into the laundry facilities.

A couple of hours.

Stacey could really use a couple of hours on the beach to

decompress and talk through her stay at Sweet Breeze. She sighed as she reached into her oversized purse for her phone. It sang out a snappy notification—literally three, sharp snaps as if someone was trying to get her attention—before she could touch it. The screen brightened, which helped her find the device, and she checked to see who'd texted.

Esther: *Beach in ten?*

"Already on my way," Stacey dictated as she thumbed out the message. She pulled off her maxi dress and changed into her bathing suit, covering it with the white, flowy shift she'd pulled on in desperation at the hotel.

She traded out the pajamas and toiletries she'd taken for her overnight stay and replaced them with sunscreen, her sunglasses, a huge, wide-brimmed hat, and her e-reader. Not that she was planning on reading. Oh, no. She had a very busy conversation ahead of her with her best friend, and the center of all the talk would be Mister Fisher Davenport himself.

———

Esther didn't arrive at their spot on the beach for twenty minutes. Usually right on time, Esther dropped her bag in a great, flustered show. "Have you seen the traffic in and out of that place?"

She didn't have to name Sweet Breeze for Stacey to know to what she was referencing. She adjusted the purple hibiscus behind her left ear and said, "It's bad right now?"

"Apparently lunchtime around here has turned into a

bloodbath for parking. I couldn't find a space to save my life. I'm all the way down by the blasted Spam Hut." She unfolded her beach chair and sank into it, righting her bag at her side and pulling out a bottle of guava lemonade. She took a long drink, as if it would somehow calm her.

"I hear you. We've filed the complaint about the traffic with the city. There's a hearing next week."

"Hearing, schmearing." Esther shook her blonde head. "I'm telling you, no one on the City Council is going to do anything about that place." It was almost like Esther thought if she said Sweet Breeze, a pack of murderous wizards would appear, summoned by the very name of "that place."

"Probably not." Stacey reclined in her beach chair, extending her bare legs out in front of her to soak up the maximum amount of vitamin D and sunshine. She watched Esther from behind her shiny sunglasses, one of her favorite activities. There was nothing more entertaining than people-watching on the beach, and Stacey had mastered it a decade ago. She could tell which couples were happy, and who had come to Getaway Bay to well, get away. From each other or from their problems at home, Stacey didn't know.

She could detect wealth from a mile away, and find those who wanted everyone to look at them, and search out those who normally blended in. They were the most interesting, and Stacey loved watching people interact with others when they thought no one was looking.

Esther smeared sunscreen over her shoulders and down her arms. Petite and powerful, she owned a private car service in the Bay area, and she really despised the traffic Sweet Breeze had brought to their quaint corner of paradise.

"Your business isn't suffering, is it?" Stacey asked. She'd thought Esther was doing quite well with the new addition to their island. After all, a swanky hotel brought high rollers with loads of cash. And people like that never drove themselves around, not even to see the sights.

"Of course not," Esther snapped, lifting her eyes to meet Stacey's behind the mirrored shades. "But everything takes twice as long." She softened, her bad mood at having to park so far away and tromp through the hot sand melting into pure curiosity. "You stayed there last night. How was it?"

Her cerulean eyes took on a hungry glow, and Stacey laughed. "Honestly, Esther, you should go." She sat up straight. "I got a free night. You should use it."

"You got a free night? At Sweet Breeze? How?"

Stacey waved her hand like it was no big deal, though she'd be spilling the whole story in seconds. "Oh, there was a mishap with the room service, and I was offered a free room. I took it."

Esther positioned her own shades over her eyes. "We should have the Beach Club there next time we meet."

The thought of having their Women's Beach Club—a secret society of women on the island who'd been burned by men, had their husbands leave them for younger, prettier women, or who had simply decided not to pursue romance —inside Sweet Breeze made Stacey burst into laughter.

"That's perfect," she said, thinking of the perfectly romantic atmosphere Sweet Breeze worked so hard to create. "Ironic, but perfect."

"We can totally order room service. Maybe we'll get more free rooms."

Somehow, Stacey didn't think so. Men like Fisher fixed problems like the one she'd had that morning. She switched her gaze to the undulating teal water of the bay, a measure of relaxation finally sighing through her. "It was a nice hotel."

"Of course it's nice," Esther said. "It cost two billion dollars to build."

"I met him, you know."

"Who?"

"The owner."

"You did?" Esther kicked sand onto Stacey's feet as she launched herself forward. "How? What was he like?"

Before Stacey could answer, another bag got dropped on the sand beside Esther. "Watch out," Tawny Loveless, the third part of their little boyfriend-less triangle, said. "There's a god walking this way."

She was part of the Women's Beach Club and claimed she didn't want or need a man in her life. But she seemed to know who all the available men on the island were, and her radar for a good-looking man was unmatched.

Stacey didn't want to look, but she found her head swiveling back the way Tawny had come. There was indeed a god walking their way, and she'd seen that gait before. Seen him before, only a couple of hours ago.

A hiss leaked from her body as it went cold. Though it was the height of summer, and the sun was practically burning everything and everyone on the beach, Stacey shivered. The tall, nearly bald man wore a dark gray rash guard that rippled with the lines of his muscles, and a bright orange pair of swim trunks.

"That's him," she said in a voice she simply meant to be

hushed but which came out with a sort of reverence she didn't understand.

"Who?" Even Esther's normally boisterous tone had softened.

"The owner of Sweet Breeze. Fisher Davenport." And he was headed directly toward Stacey herself.

FOUR

FISHER HAD *KNOWN* the redhead in fifteen-twenty-one had looked familiar. Stacey Stapleton owned Aloha Hideaway, one of the few bed and breakfast locations at Getaway Bay. He knew he'd seen her at the City Council meetings where all anyone ever did was complain about "men like him" and "hotels that big."

She'd never stepped up to the mic, but she obviously held considerable power on the island—and his own Google search had confirmed why. She was a three-generation Hawaiian business owner. Her grandfather had created a new strain of hibiscus flower, and she ran the most successful B&B in the area.

He wasn't angry at her undercover sting to spy on his hotel, and he hadn't planned on confronting her for parading around under a false name. But when he saw her trademark red hair now piled on top of her head in a messy bun, he'd thought it wise to go say hello. He was friendly and all that, and she was sitting right on the edge of the private beach for Sweet Breeze.

He hadn't seen her at any of the tourism management meetings, and someone as sharp and smart as her should've been there. Perhaps she didn't know about them.

Better to keep it that way, he told himself as he approached. He wasn't one to be shy with women, but with three of them staring at him with icy waves radiating from them, the confidence in his step died several paces away.

"Good afternoon," he said. At least his voice hadn't revealed his nerves. He glanced at the blonde and the second woman with dyed streaks in her brown hair, but his gaze was drawn back to Stacey as if her face was made of a powerful magnet. Her beauty struck him full in the chest, and he sucked in a breath that was thankfully masked by a sudden swell crashing against the beach.

"We're not on your beach," the blonde said.

"No, you're not."

"That's not why he's here." Stacey stood, her long, tan legs momentarily distracting Fisher. She wore a bright blue bikini that she filled out in all the right ways, but Fisher kept his eyes on hers as she stepped forward in bare feet on the hot sand. "I'm Stacey Stapleton."

A smirk quirked his mouth though he tried to smother it. Working with his father for seven years, Fisher had learned to show zero emotion. But he'd been out from under that hard thumb for a couple of years now, and his tough guy act had started to slip.

"I know. I can Google, you know."

She narrowed her eyes at him, not quite the reaction he'd

been going for. What he'd wanted, he still wasn't sure. He'd given up dating at the same time he gave up the shares in his father's construction firm, and he'd be the first to admit he was a bit rusty.

"I highly doubt I came up on any Google search of yours, Mister Davenport." She cocked her hip and folded her arms. If she'd been wearing anything but a bikini, the stance would've been powerful and businesslike. But with the strings and triangles of fabric, it only enhanced the curves he'd admired while dressed as a room service attendant.

"You can call me Fisher."

The woman with streaked hair scoffed, and Fisher looked at her. She looked so familiar.... He thought she maybe worked for him in some capacity, but he hadn't been to every department yet and wasn't sure.

Stacey flicked her gaze toward her friend. When she looked back at Fisher, she asked, "What do you want? I'm not giving back the free room."

He pasted a smile in place. "I just came to say hello." He spread the grin around to all the women, all of whom clearly disliked him, Stacey included. Focusing on her again, he said, "When you come, we should have breakfast together. You can tell me why you stayed at Sweet Breeze and what you liked or didn't like."

"Breakfast?" all three women chorused together. It couldn't have been any more perfect if they'd rehearsed it.

Stacey laughed, and not the flirty type of giggle Fisher suddenly wanted to hear from her. "I don't think so, *Fisher*."

"No problem," he said smoothly. "I'll simply watch for you—or Miss Moore—to check in, and then I'll send up room service." He twisted halfway as if he would walk away, then paused and turned just his head back to her, thinking about telling her he was the one who'd entered without knocking.

Deciding against it, he said, "Oh, and it would be nice if we're going to be friends that you call me by the right name."

"We aren't going to be friends," Stacey said, a flash of something in her expression that Fisher couldn't quite identify before it fled.

"Oh, I think we will." He gave them another smile, this one oozing with as much charm as he could muster, the one he used when there were expensive cameras around and reporters calling his name to look their way.

He started to walk away, the sand that came up over his sandaled feet searing his skin. He really needed to get outside more, but he could already feel the sunburn starting on his shaved scalp. *Blast Marshall and his blade-happy ways.*

"What's the right name?" Stacey called after him.

"Google it," he called over his shoulder.

———

"You'd like me to book you a room at Aloha Hideaway." Owen wasn't really asking, but his tone dripped with incredulity.

"Yes." Fisher straightened the collar on his polo. After getting fired from the room service department of his own hotel and then mulling over where he'd seen the redhead before, he'd taken some time to unwind on the beach. But the last experience he'd had there had gotten him all wound up again.

"May I ask why?"

Fisher appreciated the question from his general manager. After all, if Owen Church just blindly went about everything Fisher instructed him to do, he wouldn't be much of a general manager. He cast a glance at the man a decade his senior, trying to formulate his response without revealing that part of the reason was simply to see Stacey again.

"Part of my undercover operations," he said, hoping that would be enough. He should know it wouldn't be.

Owen cocked an eyebrow. "Sir, I thought we were doing those within our own hotel. I heard about the mishap this morning."

Fisher turned from the mirror in Owen's office. It sat down the hall and around the corner from the main lobby, far enough from the fray to provide some peace and quiet yet close enough to be summoned should the need arise. Fisher had hired the best architectural firm in commercial real estate to design Sweet Breeze and no detail had been left unattended.

"She was here to check out my building," Fisher said. "I want to see hers."

"I thought you stayed in several of the hotels before deciding on Getaway Bay."

"I did. Not the Aloha Hideaway." He glanced at his phone, where he'd done his online spying. "I read that it was the hidden jewel on the big island. My home in Getaway Bay."

Owen's dubious look remained, but he said, "Very well. Should I use your name?"

"Of course. I'm not trying to hide." Not like Jaida Moore had been.

"For tonight? They have Kalua pig on their dinner menu on Thursdays."

Fisher's mouth watered at the mere mention of the famous Hawaiian dish. "Tonight and tomorrow, if they're not booked."

Owen picked up the phone and placed the call. From the way he kept his back turned and concluded with, "I see. Let me consult his schedule," Fisher determined he would not be packing a bag and staying down the beach.

Sharp disappointment cut through him when Owen confirmed that Aloha Hideaway was full until September.

"September?" He moved around the wingback chair and slouched into it. "I don't think we've been full yet."

"There are only five rooms at Aloha Hideaway," Owen said in his best placating voice. "We have four hundred and fifty-two rooms here at Sweet Breeze, sir."

Fisher knew how many rooms his hotel had. He knew how many had been full last night—two hundred twelve— and how many were full tonight—three hundred and five. He could recall obscure details from reports and remember most of what he read. He hadn't built his empire without using his brain.

A knock sounded on the door and Owen said, "Come," his eyes still on Fisher.

A man wearing a dark suit and tie entered. "Weather report for the next week, Owen. The National Weather

Service has issued a warning for the beginning of next week. I thought you'd want to know."

Fisher sat up straighter as the report was passed from one manager to the other. He smiled at the man, glancing at his nametag—Ikaika—and memorizing it, letting the Hawaiian vowels roll around in his mind until he thought he'd get it right if he had to speak the name.

Owen flipped through the few pages of the report, not really reading it. "Thank you, Ikaika."

Ee-kai-ka. Just how Fisher would've said it. The man nodded and left the room, and Owen set the weather report down.

Fisher didn't like the way the man stared. He wasn't really glaring and he said nothing, but somehow, he'd mastered how to make Fisher squirm with a simple look.

"Are Cooper and Zach around tonight?" he asked.

"They're at their mother's."

On Maui, then. Fisher stood. He could entertain himself on a Thursday evening without Owen's teenage sons. Heck, Marshall had nightly entertainment on the pineapple plantations, and Fisher suddenly had the desire for a frozen tropical smoothie from Two Coconuts, which happened to sit just down the street.

He exited the building to a wave of heat, wondering if he'd ever get used to it. Probably not. He'd lived in Los Angeles for ten years before coming to Getaway Bay, but his mother had remarried and raised him and his two half-sisters in Michigan. Ice, snow, and wind he could deal with. Blazing heat he could barely tolerate.

Two Coconuts was a popular place to get a traditional

Hawaiian drink, with or without alcohol, and Fisher had never seen it without a line extending toward the street. Even at nine o'clock in the morning, Two Coconuts was blending smoothies and rimming glasses in sugar. Probably because it was scorching hot by dawn.

Fisher joined the line, glad he'd given up his suit for the day. The way things were going, he thought he might leave it hanging in his closet until Monday morning. Yes, a nice, long weekend without the pressures of dealing with anything hotel-related sounded like exactly what he needed.

"Thank you, Leilani. You're the best." The female voice sang through Fisher's soul and he didn't have to look far to catch sight of those red locks that had been plaguing him all day. What were the chances he'd see her for the third time in one day?

No, he thought. *The fourth.* Just because he'd pretended it to be Raymond Royce's first day on room service didn't mean he hadn't encountered Stacey four times now.

This time, instead of wearing a turban on her head, or a gorgeous maxi dress, or a stunning bikini, she juggled crates of drinks with curly straws coming out of the top. No way she was going far with those, and while nothing could satisfy Fisher's thirst except for the Maui Wowi—pineapple juice, frozen mango and strawberries, with just a hint of lime in the background—he suddenly had a hunger that needed to be curbed first.

"Hey," he said, stepping out of line and darting toward Stacey. "Looks like you could use a hand."

She looked at him, bobbling the crates when she recognized him. "I'm fine." But her bare foot caught in the sand and she stumbled forward, trying to catch her balance.

Fisher didn't think; he lunged forward and only had a split second to decide if he should save the woman or the drinks. Judging by how much money a crateful of drinks cost from Two Coconuts, Fisher grabbed the bottom crate with both hands, trying to somehow catch Stacey too.

He could do a lot of things—run a mile in under seven minutes, solve a Rubix cube without ever touching it, calculate mentally how much interest he made each month on the money sitting in his numerous bank accounts—but he couldn't save Stacey from sprawling face-first in the sand.

FIVE

EMBARRASSMENT FILLED every cell and crevice of Stacey's body. Her eyes burned and she absolutely hated having sand in her teeth.

"You okay?" Fisher's round, bass voice filled her ears. Hands touched her arms and helped her up, but they weren't his. Such a shame.

She shook her head as much to get the traitorous thoughts out as to remove the sand from her hair. "I'm all right."

"I saved the drinks." He set the crate of Island Surfers on the sand beside her and scanned her. "It was you or them. Sorry if I chose wrong." He glanced down, and somehow the gesture made him adorable instead of handsome. Soft instead of hard. Approachable instead of intimidating. The casual gym shorts and plain navy T-shirt helped with all of the above.

"No, it's fine," she said. "They're for my dinner guests,

and they are pricey." Stacey loved the orange sherbet, pineapple juice, and coconut cream concoctions, and no one made them better than Leilani. She always worked her family's stand on Thursday nights, and Stacey had added the Island Surfers to the menu to entice people to book an extra night at Aloha Hideaway.

She brushed as much sand from her clothes as possible, wishing the beach would swallow her whole. Her face felt as hot as the surface of the sun and was probably the same color as her hair. She pushed it off her face with as much grace as she could muster and exhaled.

"Thank you." The words were hard to get out, but they sounded genuine. She reached for the crate, but Fisher bent and beat her to it.

"I'll carry them for you."

"You don't have to."

"I want to see your bed and breakfast." He stepped and his long strides put quite a bit of distance between them in only a few seconds. "You coming?"

Stacey watched for another breath, wondering what other choice she had. Anger rose to the top of her head and she stomped after him. "You can't come in my place."

"Why not? You stayed at mine."

"I have a maximum capacity and I've met it for tonight."

Fisher eyed the crate. "Looks like sixteen drinks. Is that maximum capacity for Aloha Hideaway?"

It was actually twenty-two, but Stacey kept that information to herself.

"Higher or lower?"

"If you want to see inside, get a reservation."

"I tried." He glanced at her, seemingly enjoying this game. Stacey, however, was not. "Did you know you're booked through September?"

"I did." Panic built in her chest with every step they took that led them closer to Aloha Hideaway. "You can see pictures online."

"Ah, but it's not the same as actually *being* there, is it?" He gave her a smirk mixed with a smile. "Did you figure out my name?"

"Surprisingly, it's not something Google knows. Siri either. I even tried Alexa. Nothing."

"Hm. You're a smart woman. You'll figure it out."

"Why don't you just tell me?" They'd passed the private beach for Sweet Breeze and now walked along a narrow strip of sand between the bay and a thicket of trees. On the other side of those were her hibiscus gardens. She'd been cultivating them and having Marge clear space for weddings. This was the first year they'd been ready to book, but business had been slow so far.

"What's the fun in that?" Fisher asked, adjusting the crate.

The hedge her grandfather had spent years trimming came into view, with the gate to Aloha Hideaway just another hundred yards ahead. She darted in front of Fisher. "I can take it from here."

He stopped and looked down at her. It was stupidly unfair that he was so tall. So handsome. As Tawny had said after he'd walked away on the beach earlier that day, just because he was drop-dead gorgeous didn't mean he couldn't be nice too. But in Stacey's experience, those two things—

good looks and kindness—didn't normally come in the same package. Of course, at this point in her life, she wasn't even interested in the nice guys.

With only three years until she turned forty, Stacey had come to terms with the course of her life. She had an amazing family-like staff at Aloha Hideaway. Excellent friends in her Women's Beach Club. A thriving business. No man was needed.

"I'm sure you can," Fisher said, taking an extra step into her, crowding her, invading her personal space.

She fell back a pace.

"But I want to help, Stacey. I'll just take them into the kitchen and go right back out. I promise. You'll find I'm extraordinarily good at *deliveries*." A twinkle sat in those impossibly blue eyes, something so playful and bright that Stacey's first inclination was to smile.

She held back the action as pieces clicked around in her mind. "Deliveries?" She sucked in a breath, her mouth widened, and she covered it with one still-sandy hand. "You were the room service attendant?"

He glanced over his shoulder like there would be someone standing there to overhear. His feet shifted in the sand, and while Stacey went barefoot almost everywhere on the island, she'd noticed that Fisher always wore footwear. Both times she'd seen him, it had been a pair of brown leather flip flops.

"I sort of do undercover...excursions at my hotel."

"Excursions?" The word made no sense to Stacey.

"Sweet Breeze is a big place. A lot of people. Many moving parts." He settled his weight on his back foot. "I...I work undercover in each of the respective departments to see how things operate. See how my employees are faring. That kind of thing."

Stacey gazed up at him, wonder traveling through her with the speed of cold molasses. Who was this man? He didn't sound like anything the articles she'd read about The Davenport Development Group. They had a nasty reputation for skirting the laws in the cities where they built, fabricating permits if they'd "forgotten" to get them, and paying their employees basement-bottom wages.

She could not imagine any of their top-level executives going undercover—or even caring how their employees were faring.

"That's...nice," she managed to say. She looked at her phone to give herself a moment of distance, a second to find clarity of thought. "Look, my dinner service just started. I need those Island Surfers inside."

"Great." Fisher stepped around her, somehow knowing that the gate would take him right up to the historic building she'd transformed into the Aloha Hideaway. He passed through it, and she had to take two steps for every one of his.

"Straight back," she said as he climbed the few steps to the porch.

"This place is great," he said, glancing around. "Feels exactly like my home here on Getaway Bay." He tossed her a dazzling smile, and she rolled her eyes.

"Straight back," she repeated.

He entered the lobby, and he appeared to be watching a tennis match with the way his head swiveled from left to right and back. Betty waved from the door on the back right, and Fisher headed that direction.

"Island Surfers," he announced as Betty held the door open for him.

"Thank you," Stacey said, pulling the drinks out of the crate as soon as he'd put it on the stainless steel table in the middle of the kitchen.

"Need help serving them?" He picked up one drink.

Stacey almost swatted it out of his hand, but she had fourteen guests eating dinner tonight, and that was *her* Island Surfer. After getting a mouthful of sand in front of the best looking man on the island, Stacey needed it even though it was nonalcoholic. The other was for Betty, who'd stayed on tonight after Dillan had called in with a sick four-year-old.

"No." Stacey spoke in the firmest voice she possessed, and carefully took the drink from Fisher. With the other hand, she pressed against Fisher's chest, moving him backward toward the door. "You can go away now."

"You sure?" He moved, his steps backward sure, though she was certain that if he resisted, there'd be no way she could get him out of her bed and breakfast.

"Absolutely sure. I've carried those drinks from Two Coconuts for over a year. We're good here. Why don't you go…I don't know. Run some towels through the washing machine?"

Fisher held up both hands in a gesture of surrender, a chuckle rumbling his chest—where she still had her hand planted against the hard muscles there. She pulled her hand back like his body had caught fire.

He continued backward for a few steps, casting his eyes all around the lobby, which thankfully, had just been cleaned top to bottom in preparation for the upcoming storm. If guests had to stay indoors, Stacey liked to make it as comfortable and pleasant for them as possible.

Fisher turned and walked forward, and Stacey *really* needed to stop watching him walk out of her life.

———

The next morning, Stacey meandered through her hibiscus gardens, hoping the storm that was supposed to arrive in a few days wouldn't ruin the crop that was almost ready to harvest. Henry and Hugs, her two schnauzers, pranced through the foliage, playing a game with one another she didn't understand.

"Perhaps we should take these rows early," she said to Marge, who worked further down the aisle, her long fingers lovingly stroking the delicate petals of a plant. "I don't want to lose them to the storm."

"Is there room in the refrigeration unit?" Marge straightened and glided forward. She reminded Stacey of a butterfly. A tall, graceful, always-wears-her-dirty-blonde-hair-in-a-ponytail type of butterfly.

"I have Samar from Bay Tours coming to get everything I've got this afternoon." Stacey listened to the breeze as it drifted through the gardens, disturbing the palm fronds above her head. She glanced up, a smile forming on her face. A calm sense of security enveloped her, and her eyes drifted closed. Stacey imagined herself floating on the current, letting it push her, pull her, take her out across the bay where no human had ever flown before.

"Can I talk to you for a second?" The strong male voice punctured her fantasy and brought her crashing back to Earth.

She spun to find Fisher Unknown-Last-Name standing in her gardens. Her heart bumped against her ribcage in a strange pattern, almost like it was trying to spell out *e-x-c-i-t-e-d* in Morse Code.

She cinched her arms across her chest, as if trying to hide her heartbeat. "This is private property."

Nothing seemed to ruffle him, and even his polos looked like they cost hundreds of dollars. He certainly hadn't bought the shades of blue, plaid polo off the rack at the department store on the other side of the island. No, he probably had them flown in from Milan or Paris or somewhere exotic where polos were made.

He gave her an easy smile that did unfair things to her pulse and raised the temperature in the shady garden by a few degrees. "I inquired at the front desk, and your super friendly receptionist said I could find you out here." He glanced behind her where Marge and the dogs were.

Stacey followed his gaze, but Marge was bent over, holding very still, her ear near the plants. Stacey shifted her feet to position herself between Marge and Fisher. He didn't need to know that her horticulturist thought she could talk to flowers. Her schnauzers couldn't be seen, but Stacey knew they wouldn't leave the gardens.

She focused back on Fisher. "You found me. What did you need?"

His grin faded. "I wanted to invite you to the tourism management meeting on Tuesday."

Stacey flinched, unsure of why. "Tourism management meeting?" Her voice sounded like she'd sucked in a lungful of helium. "I've lived on this island my whole life. I didn't know there was such a meeting."

"I figured as much," he said. "I've never seen you there, and you seem like the kind of...." His eyes flicked down her body and back to her face. "Business owner who would attend every week."

"I just opened the B&B a few years ago."

"Five years, according to Google."

Anger flashed through her. "I hate the Internet sometimes."

He chuckled and the sound joined the wind still lilting through the trees. "It can be a pain, I'll agree. Did you figure out my name?"

"No," she said. "But I know your father is Stanley Davenport, of the Davenport Development Group. And that company is what's listed on all your legal documents, building permits, the whole nine yards. My assumption was at least intelligent."

"I never said you weren't intelligent." That quick glance at her again, and Stacey wished she'd come out to the gardens in more than a skin-tight pair of leggings and an old T-shirt with faded emojis on it.

"Quite the opposite, in fact."

Stacey conceded the point. He had called her smart a couple of times now. She wished the compliment didn't warm her so completely. She was not interested in starting a relationship of any kind with Fisher. Not a friendship. Not anything in the romantic realm, even if he was devilishly good-looking and had shown professionalism and kindness whenever she encountered him.

"Perhaps you could just tell me your name," she said. "It is Fisher, yes?"

"Fisher is my first name."

"And your father is Stanley Davenport?"

His expression tightened; his blue eyes darkened. "Unfortunately."

So she needed to search for who his mother was, what her last name was. That was probably the name Fisher went by these days. The thought of sitting in her private suite, huddled over the laptop while she performed a fruitless—and meaningless search—with Henry and Hugs at her side, didn't appeal to her.

"So what's your last name?"

He regarded her with the coolness of a man who had a lot of money. Someone who was used to getting things done his way. Fisher also seemed childlike, eager to please, vulnerable beneath the layers of his wealth.

"How about I tell you over dinner?"

Stacey opened her mouth to reply, but her mind went blank. She wasn't used to coming up with nothing. She always had a witty comeback, the perfect parting quip. But now, her eyes searched his face rapidly, looking for any clue that he was kidding. There didn't seem to be any.

"I serve dinner here seven days a week," she said. Such a commitment had cost her a couple of relationships with men who didn't like to come in second to her bed and breakfast.

Which had been fine with Stacey. She didn't want a man so superficial anyway, and those relationships had dissolved before they'd really taken root.

"Can one buy a spot at the table?"

"I'm full until September."

"Surely every guest doesn't eat here every night."

No, they didn't, but Stacey pressed the answer behind her closed lips.

"So how much?" He put his hands in the pockets of his khaki shorts, the kind rich men wore on the golf course, confident he'd be eating at her table that night.

"Friday is a fish fry," she said. "It's expensive."

"How much?" he repeated.

"There will be fourteen other people at the table."

He tilted his head to the side, the third iteration of his question obvious.

Stacey wanted more information about the tourism meeting, his name, his hotel…him.

Fear rose in her like a tidal wave, the kind that had engulfed her and crushed her in the past. Twice. She couldn't go through that emotional pain again. She'd found happiness in her bed and breakfast, her two dogs and a cat, her staff, her Women's Beach Club.

She did not need a man, even if he was handsome, charming, and rich. Even if he stood in her gardens, promising her business information that could change her bottom line or a glimpse into the imperfections of his life he obviously worked to hide.

"I'll ask Tayla," he said. "She was bubbly and bright, and I'm sure she'll know if I can purchase a seat for dinner, and on which night." Fisher turned, and Stacey would not let him walk away from her again even if she enjoyed the view.

She scrambled for something to keep him there. "I don't serve lunch," came out of her mouth.

He turned back but only halfway. "Lunch?"

She shrugged as Henry the schnauzer came to sit at her feet. "I'm always available for lunch."

SIX

FISHER'S SURPRISE couldn't be contained behind the mask he'd put on as soon as he'd seen Stacey in the garden. He couldn't believe he'd asked her to dinner, and he wasn't surprised by her resistance. She wasn't exactly cold to him, but she hadn't been warm either.

So when his eyebrows went up, she didn't act like his reaction was strange.

"Lunch?" he repeated as if he wasn't familiar with the midday meal.

"I usually skip breakfast," she said with a small half-shrug. "We can work around your schedules—our schedules."

"When?" he asked. He'd go right now though it was only nine-fifteen. His day had started early in the bagelry, the only one of it's kind on the island, located on the second floor of Sweet Breeze. They served bagels in every variety, including a few tropical ones Fisher had never seen on the mainland. And apparently, mango guava bagels had to be started at three AM, because the fifteen-hundred-square-foot shop had been packed by six-thirty that morning.

"Whenever," she said, a totally non-committal answer.

He didn't want to pick when they could go to lunch. He wanted her to set the pace, show him how eager she was to go out with him, reveal a little bit about her lifestyle. Though, finding her with her horticulturalist in the gardens when check-out was in full swing said quite a lot. Stacey ran a tight ship from what he'd seen, but everyone was friendly, professional, and knowledgeable.

Fisher rotated his shoulder slightly, easing the ache that remained from so much kneading that morning. He'd snuck away after the crowds had died, which was about nine o'clock. The manager said they usually had a lull until ten-thirty or so, when people then decided they'd like a bagel for lunch. The shop closed at three in the afternoon, and took anything they hadn't sold that day down to the beach to sell straight to customers on the sand.

"I'm busy today," he said, even though he wasn't. Not really. He had meetings and phone calls and probably something to talk about with Owen. But it could all be rescheduled. He just didn't want her to think he was immediately available. Maybe he didn't want to appear warmer than she was. He wasn't sure.

"Oh, me too," she said.

"Tomorrow?"

"Saturday?"

He grinned at her. "Yeah, tomorrow's Saturday." Honestly, Fisher didn't usually know what day of the week it was. They were all the same to him, except for where he'd be spending his time working. However, he and Owen had decided to keep the undercover hours on weekdays only, so he did know tomorrow he could sleep in without being late to the laundry, the kitchens, or housekeeping.

His phone buzzed before she could confirm or deny, and the name of his general manager flashed on the screen in red when Fisher pulled the device from his pocket. His heart bumped up into his throat as alarm spread through him. "Excuse me." He lifted his phone to indicate he was getting a call and turned his back on her.

"Owen?"

"We've had four separate complaints from pool seven," he said. "Apparently there are some rowdy guests causing problems."

Fisher was already walking back through the gardens the way he'd come. "Call security."

"I did; they're there. The guests are refusing to leave, citing that they've paid and they deserve to stay. They've demanded to see the owner."

"I'm on my way." He hung up and turned back to see Stacey watching him. He lifted his hand in a wave he hoped could say *Sorry, I'll talk to you later*, but she ducked away from him as if she didn't want to be caught staring.

He kept his eyes on the red hair that tumbled over her shoulders and down her back, probably for too long. She didn't turn around, and he forced himself to hurry back to the Sweet Breeze to take care of business.

Something told him not to leave Aloha Hideaway without a way to get in contact with Stacey, so he took a quick detour toward the front desk. Thankfully, there was no line like there had been earlier when he'd stopped by to inquire about Stacey's whereabouts.

"Mister DuPont," Tayla said, her smile slipping easily across her face. "Did you not find her in the gardens? I could radio to find out where she is." She had one hand on the radio when Fisher shook his head.

"No, I found her, but we got interrupted. I wonder...." He searched the counter for a pen and paper, but Tayla had everything tucked away neatly. "Could I leave my number for her?" He gazed into the woman's sky blue eyes evenly.

The blonde didn't bat any of her false eyelashes. "Of course." She reached into a drawer and handed him a white sticky note with purple flowers in the corner. "Write it there and I'll take it to her personal suite myself."

Fisher had a half-dozen questions build in his mind at the mention of Stacey's personal suite. He hadn't gotten the impression she lived on-site. But his phone buzzed again, and the urgency to get back to his own hotel burned like fire.

He scratched out his number and nodded at Tayla. "Thank you."

"Sure thing, Mister DuPont."

He hurried out to his car and around the curve in the island to his hotel. He liked walking the beach as much as the next person, but he'd had enough sand between his toes for a while.

Owen met him at the pool elevators like Fisher was wearing a tracking device. "There are three of them, sir. Security is still at number seven and the other guests have been relocated to other pools."

Fisher wished he wore his expensive suit, but perhaps showing up looking like a regular guy would be beneficial in this case. "Drinking?"

"They are definitely drunk."

"From our enterprises? Or did they bring in outside alcohol?"

"None of our bartenders have served them anything." Owen handed him a single sheet of paper. "The complaints."

Fisher nodded and skimmed the report as the elevator ascended toward the upper levels. The top of the hotel had been built like a pyramid, with smaller and smaller square footage so the footprint could accommodate pools on five different levels. Pool seven was on the twenty-seventh floor, and Fisher had his own private pool on the twenty-eighth, with a massive pool on the roof of his penthouse that provided the best swimming experience in the Pacific region. At least that was what *Travel, the Magazine* had said. Fisher hadn't even paid them to, and their already good business had been better since the article came out six months ago.

Level twenty-seven had three pools, and seven faced the bay. Four security guards stood in a line, shoulder-to-shoulder, with their backs to the view. The three men sat facing them, the pool between them. The scent of rum lingered in the air.

"Gentlemen," he said, and all three of them turned toward him. "I hear you wanted to speak with me." He sized them up as they stood. Each had seen time in a gym. Each had drunk too much today already. Each didn't seem like the kind to scare away families with rowdy behavior.

"We have a right to be swimmin'," one of them said, and Fisher detected a decidedly Southern accent.

"That's true," Fisher said. "So what's the problem?"

"We were told we hadta leave," he slurred. The other two had obviously elected him their leader at some point.

"There is to be no alcohol consumed in this pool," he said, pointing to a sign that clearly stated the rules. "Inside or outside alcohol. It's a family pool."

The man turned toward the sign and frowned as if he hadn't been informed of this rule. When he looked back at Fisher, the confusion rode in his dark eyes.

"In fact," Fisher continued. "Alcohol can only be consumed in pools one and two, on level twenty-four. Not only that, but it must be purchased at one of the four bars there. You can't bring in your own." He shrugged and lifted up his hands in surrender. "You'll get my alcohol permit revoked, guys. You understand I can't violate the terms I've agreed to with the state of Hawaii."

Several beats of silence passed, and Fisher thought it probably wasn't a good idea to talk legal jargon with drunk men.

"Level twenty-four isn't open-air," another man said. He seemed much more lucid than the first man. His cold, blue eyes watched Fisher.

"Another legality I can't help," Fisher said. He had to have proper containment if alcohol was going to be served hundreds of feet in the air. The last thing anyone wanted was someone drinking too much and stumbling off the side of the building. "I'm afraid it's pool one or two, fellas. Of course, you're always welcome to come back here when you've sobered up."

"We've paid to stay here," the first man said.

"I'm not asking you to leave the hotel," Fisher explained. "But if I have to get the police involved, I might not be able to keep you here. They'll probably want to take you to the station for questioning...." He let the threat hang there, and the least drunk of the men touched the first man's arm.

"Let's go down to twenty-four," he said.

"My men would be happy to make sure you arrive there safely." Fisher indicated his security guards should come forward now. They moved like robots, splitting in half and coming around the pool two by two. He mentally added the security department to the list of places he still needed to visit as part of his undercover work.

"And guys," he said when they were surrounded by the security detail. "If I find out you're drinking anything but what my bartenders serve you, that's grounds to be escorted off the property, whether you've paid or not. You signed your name to that when you checked in."

"We haven't been," the second man said, and again Fisher knew when he was being lied to. He nodded anyway and let security go with the men to the pool elevator.

He relaxed as soon as the doors slid closed. Sitting on a nearby chaise, he locked eyes with Owen. "I hate this part of the job."

"You're exceptionally skilled at it, Fisher."

Fisher looked away, out over the aqua water of Getaway Bay. "I wish I never had need to be." But working with his father for seven years had taught Fisher a lot about how to deal with conflict.

"I believe you have dinner and drinks in the conference room on level eleven tonight. Yes?"

Fisher nodded absently, though the thought of meeting with his fellow Nine-0's usually had him full of anticipation. It was the one place he didn't have to pretend to be something different than who or what he was.

"Are you going to stay here for a while, sir?" Owen had already moved over to the elevator bank and pushed the button.

Fisher stood at the same time his phone buzzed. He pulled it out of his pocket to find an unknown number and part of a message—*Hey, it's Stacey. You sneaky little*—at the top of his screen. It slipped back up and out of sight, leaving only a chat bubble in his notification bar.

"Yes," he said, deciding on the spot. "I'm going to relax here for a few minutes." He waited until Owen had gotten on the elevator and the doors had closed before finding a soft chair in the shade. He had no sunscreen with him and the last thing he needed was his head, neck, and ears to get burnt because he was distracted with the woman down the beach.

She hadn't left his mind for a moment since he'd met her wearing that maxi dress.

Hey, it's Stacey. You sneaky little fox. Leaving your number with Tayla. Do you know how much explaining I had to do? Thanks a lot MISTER DUPONT.

Fisher tipped his head back and laughed, the foreign

sound meeting his own ears. He wasn't sure when he'd last laughed like this, but it had been an exceptionally long time.

Fox? he typed out. *So you think I'm foxy?*

I think you apparently only tell certain people your last name. And it's not your mother's.

It is my mother's. She remarried when I was eight. When my father

Fisher stared at the words, wondering if they were too personal. He didn't share his past with many people. Heck, he shared very little of his present with others. A select few —Owen, the members of the Nine-0 club, his mother. That was about it.

Did he want to add Stacey to the list?

Fisher had dated plenty of women in his twenties. Since dedicating himself to Sweet Breeze, though, he'd gotten away from the constant need to meet for drinks, the business dinners that always turned casual. Now he conducted all his meetings from a board room, no food or drink in sight. It had been cleansing, a fresh start, a different way of doing business than his father had done it.

I also think you're foxy.

Stacey's text jumpstarted Fisher's heart in a way it hadn't been touched before. He'd never thought he'd had a void in his life only a woman could fill, but staring at those five words, he definitely felt a hollowness inside him that money, friends, and the best hotel in the western hemisphere hadn't been able to ease.

So he finished his text. *It is my mother's. She remarried when I was eight. When my father abandoned us and stopped sending money when I was ten, I took my step-father's name. He's a good man, and I like being a DuPont.*

Employing his bravery and hoping Stacey could read between the lines, he sent the message.

———

"Who have you been texting?" Marshall, all six-feet-two-inches of him, stopped next to Fisher.

He looked up from his phone and shoved it in his pocket when he caught Marshall looking. "No one."

"Right. You haven't spoken hardly a word tonight, and that's not like you." Marshall opened a bottle of seltzer water and turned to survey the crowd.

Crowd wasn't really the right word. The Hawaii Nine-0 club only had nine members total, and only seven had come tonight. They sat on expensive couches and sipped expensive waters and talked and laughed.

Fisher usually loved the Nine-0 get-togethers, especially when he hosted at Sweet Breeze. No one else had seemed to notice his lack of socialization. Of course Marshall would. Since coming to Getaway Bay five years ago, Fisher and Marshall had been friends. Marshall had asked Fisher to look through his bank statements for discrepancies his accountants hadn't found, and Fisher had found the problem in less than an hour.

They'd been inseparable since. Fisher trusted Marshall explicitly, and Marshall did the same for Fisher. Marshall hadn't dated in the time Fisher had known him, and one of the underlying principles of the Nine-0 club was that relationships weren't fair game unless a member brought them up. No questions asked.

So Marshall shouldn't have asked his question, because Fisher certainly wouldn't have spent the last two hours texting his mother. And Marshall was in the room.

"Ah, I see." Marshall took a long drink from his bottle. "Well, Ira's dying to ask our opinion on something, and I told him I'd see if I could pull you away from your...." He glanced at Fisher, his dark eyes full of sparkle and knowledge. "Mother."

"Right. Let's go see what he needs." Fisher let Marshall go first, and then he pulled his phone out of his pocket and silenced it, trying not to care that he had three new messages and he knew they were all from Stacey.

He'd been using his phone for business for years, but he honestly had no idea flirting could be so much fun with someone who wasn't even in the same room. Their conversation could wait. If there was one thing Fisher had gotten good at over the years, it was compartmentalizing.

It seemed like everyone realized that Fisher was finally focused on their meeting, and they gathered around Ira, who sat in the middle of a sleek leather couch. Beside him sat Tyler Rigby, the man Fisher considered his second best friend. Tyler had taught Fisher how to surf, how to spend a whole day on the beach doing nothing, how to find all the hole-in-the-wall places on the island so he could truly experience Hawaiian culture.

Today, Tyler seemed a bit more tired than usual, with darker circles under his playboy blue eyes than lying around warranted. A past professional poker player with billions in the bank, Tyler had retired to the island for anonymity and a slower way of life. He had the slow way of life down, and Fisher hadn't seen him do a day's work in the four years since he, Marshall, and Fisher had formed the Nine-0 club.

"So, Ira." Fisher flashed him a smile. "Marshall says you've got something to talk to us about."

Ira Johnson owned the largest fracking company out of west Texas, and he split his time between Hawaii and the Lone Star State, which he claimed was much more tolerable in the winter than the summer.

"Investments," Ira said, the topic of many of these meetings, which could be called by anyone and the location of which rotated all the time. It wasn't like they had people trying to crash their club, but it felt more meaningful to keep it secret, as if the wealth of the people in the room could be easily hidden.

Fisher kept his attention on the conversation, taking in the companies the others talked about—including Ira's own Johnson-Encarta Energy—as possibilities for new investment opportunities that had less risk than the more traditional routes. Fisher certainly wasn't hurting for cash, but he did like being smart with his money, trying new things, and making informed judgments.

So he participated, though half his thoughts lingered on the last thing he'd read from Stacey. They'd been playing a form of Would You Rather, and it had deviated to picking something from a list as their favorite.

Do you like blondes, brunettes, or redheads best?

SEVEN

"NINE-ONE-ONE?" Esther's voice on the other end of the line was partly asleep and partly pissed off. "At seven-fifteen on a Saturday?"

"Oh, don't tell me you haven't been up since five-thirty." Stacey had been, trying to arrange her body into strange animal-named positions that her limbs didn't seem to like. She hadn't been able to sleep well after Fisher's final text last night.

"I haven't," Esther said, though the words carried the hint of a lie. "I hired a weekend manager, remember?"

Stacey had not remembered that. "Sorry," she said. "I have a little…situation I need help with."

Shifting came through the line, almost like Esther was moving blankets and sheets to the side. Perhaps she really was still in bed. "The help of the whole Beach Club?"

I've always had a huge thing for redheads. Never dated one. Maybe that'll change this summer.

"Apparently," Stacey said, feeling a glow inside her like someone had stuck a light bulb next to her heart and flipped it on. He'd gone text-silent for a while, and she figured he'd gotten busy after a few hours of texting her. She couldn't expect the owner of Sweet Breeze to have nothing to occupy his time, and when he'd finally responded hours later, it was to only one of her questions.

Didn't matter. They had a lunch date on the horizon, and Stacey had no idea how to deal with it. Thus, the emergency text that went out to the Women's Beach Club.

"All right." Esther sighed out the two words. "I'll see you in an hour."

"I'll have pastries!" Stacey hung up and left her suite, the cold stones of the hallway welcome against her feet. The windows in the lobby let in the breeze, and she felt lucky to be able to actually live in the tropical paradise so many people spent so much money to come visit.

But she didn't have time for her reflections. Today, she needed to get as many carbs and as much pineapple juice as she could and be ready to hit her ladies with...the lunch date.

Her stomach twittered as she left through the front door of Aloha Hideaway and went to her car in the small parking lot bordered with trees. She ran through ways to tell them about Fisher, hoping they wouldn't chop her from the group on the spot.

"Of course they won't," she told herself upon returning to Aloha Hideaway with the required items. She'd asked to meet on her private beach, something she rarely did because of her guests, but she also didn't want to be overheard this morning.

The close proximity also allowed her to setup a small folding table for the refreshments, and she'd just slid the plastic cups from their bag when Esther arrived.

"You're early even." Stacey opened the pink pastry boxes from Singapore Sweets, which totally didn't sound like a French la patisserie, but that totally was. "I got you the nutella cronut."

"Good thing." Esther liked to act grumpy, but Stacey could tell from the impeccable makeup and miles of blonde curls that her friend had not been woken less than an hour ago. She bit into the cronut, sending powdered sugar toward the sand and a moan of satisfaction into the air.

Stacey smiled at her and set up the few beach chairs she had. Esther dropped into one, a cup of pineapple juice in one hand. "I came early to get the scoop."

"No scoops." Stacey shook her head. "You'll find out when everyone else does."

"Oh, come on." Esther licked a smidge of white sugar from the back of her hand. "Are you really going to stick to that stupid Club rule?"

"Um, you came up with that stupid Club rule, remember?"

"When I had a broken heart." Esther took another bite of her pastry.

"Well, I'm sticking to it."

"What about a hint?" she asked around the layers of fried dough and nutella-flavored pastry crème.

"If I give you a hint, you'll know the whole story. I can't

tell it twice." Number one, she didn't have time. Number two, she didn't want to be booted from her own club before she could get their help.

One by one, the other ladies of the Women's Beach Club arrived. Tawny took the spinach and egg croissant Stacey had bought just for her. She already had her bikini and cover-up on, and Stacey had a flash of jealousy over her beach yoga profession. She of all the ladies should be on Stacey's side, since Tawny worked for Sweet Breeze and thus, Fisher DuPont.

Should've asked her his last name, Stacey thought, immediately banishing the idea. If she'd gone to Tawny and asked about Fisher, red flags would've been raised much sooner than this meeting.

Winnie Broadhead bypassed the juice and loaded up on sweets. "How did you know I needed this today?" she asked, tossing her black braids over her shoulder and balancing her two plain glazed doughnuts on her knee while she tied her hair back. Stacey loved Winnie's hair, and wished she had the ability to weave threads into her hair, wear exotic flowers and actually look exotic.

Though she wasn't even close to the only dark-skinned woman on the island, Winnie was the most beautiful. Her scumbag of a husband had left her for their housekeeper a few years ago, and Winnie had taken her alimony and opened Hibiscus Ink, which had quickly become the busiest tattoo and piercing parlor on the island.

Ronnie Clifford, Willow Thompson, and Sasha Redding arrived, and once everyone had taken a few bites of their treats and exchanged hellos, their gazes all fell on Stacey. She still hadn't figured out what to say, so she stuffed another bite of lemon-filled cronut into her mouth.

"Come on," Esther said, sensing the stall. "You got us here. Tell us what the situation is and how we can help."

Stacey drew in a deep breath and took a couple swallows of juice. "I got asked out to lunch, and I said yes." Maybe she could make it through the meeting without disclosing that her date was none other than the billionaire bachelor determined to put all other overnight venues out of business with his monstrosity of a hotel. She could actually hear herself saying those words, as she'd said them before....

She glanced around at the other girls. "And I need to know what to do on a date, because I haven't been out in over four years."

"An official date?" Winnie asked.

"Yes, ma'am. Lunch. Today." Stacey wished she wasn't so excited to spend more time with Fisher. Wished she hadn't quite sworn off men so completely for so long. Okay, maybe she wasn't too sorry about that. She'd needed the male break, and it had done wonders for her self-esteem and her business.

"Who's the date with?" Esther asked, going right for the bullseye.

Stacey gave her a cool look. "Does that matter?"

"Yes," she said, along with several other choruses of "yeah," and "Sure does," from Tawny.

Stacey focused on her, sending a mental plea for Tawny to help her out on this one. "Fine. It's Fisher DuPont."

The beach went quiet, even the waves taking a momentary break and the breeze dying for a moment. In that heartbeat of soundlessness, Stacey felt detached from her body, like she really was floating away on an air current the way she'd dreamed of doing yesterday morning.

"The owner of Sweet Breeze?" Tawny asked, followed closely by, "The billionaire?" from Winnie, and "I can't believe it," from Esther.

"He's...cute," Stacey said with a shrug. "We've talked a few times, and he seems smart and friendly, and—"

"Yeah, of course he's smart and friendly." Esther gave her a pointed look. "He didn't become one of the wealthiest men in the world by being a stupid jerk."

"So we're going to lunch somewhere he promises will be authentic and amazing. I don't know what to talk about."

"Are you considering starting a relationship with him?" Winnie asked, her dark-as-coal eyes curious with a horrified edge.

"I don't know," Stacey admitted. She couldn't tell them she'd barely been able to sleep because she'd been thinking about holding his hand.

"Of course she isn't," Esther said, her eyes never leaving Stacey's. "She's going to find out more about his hotel. She stayed there on Thursday, remember?" Only then did she sweep her piercing blue eyes around the group.

Stacey couldn't vocalize anything. She *had* thought of using the lunch to get a bit more espionage done on Sweet Breeze, but it had been a fleeting thought, pushed aside easily by the breadth of Fisher's shoulders and the dazzling quality of straight-teeth smile.

A few of the women nodded, but Tawny said, "I think he's a nice guy," with a shrug. "For what it's worth. I know you've had your heart broken a couple of times, but he seems good at fixing things."

Esther threw Tawny a dirty look. "What?" she asked. "Do we really think we're all going to stay single forever?"

A pang of sadness hit Stacey in the chest. Poor Tawny. She'd had her heart ripped out, shredded, and stuffed back inside a time or two. Or three. But she hadn't given up on the idea of true love the way some of the other women had —Stacey herself included.

Until now.

Until Fisher.

Was she really considering a romantic relationship with him? She thought of the slow warmth she'd felt in the gardens, and she knew she'd entertained the idea seriously.

"Yes," Winnie said. "I'm going to stay single forever. I have no desire to give away half of everything I've built with Hibiscus Ink."

"Same here," Esther said. "I thought that was the whole point of this group."

"The group is for support," Tawny said, and Stacey stayed out of the conversation. Truth was, she had started the group as sort of a scorned women club, only allowing members who'd sworn off men and dating in general. "And Stacey needs support to know what to do on her date today."

"It's okay," she said, trying to ease some of the tension between her best friends. "I'll figure it out."

A few seconds of silence passed. "Just be yourself," Ronnie said. "He obviously already likes what he sees."

"Find out what you can about his on-site restaurants," Sasha said.

"Maybe see if he'll put flyers for the tattoo parlor in his rooms," Winnie said.

"And who does his car service," Esther added.

Stacey let them plot how she was going to use her lunch to discover and exploit all of Fisher DuPont's weaknesses and secrets. But she'd seized onto Ronnie's advice first. *Just be yourself.*

She could do that.

Couldn't she?

———

Stacey stared at herself in the mirror. "This is as good as it's going to get." Her hair hadn't quite cooperated the way she would've liked. But the front had held the curl, and she wasn't planning on turning her back on Fisher during lunch.

She'd chosen a bright blue sun dress that skimmed the tops of her knees, with wide shoulder straps and a huge, white floral print covering the fabric. It was one of her favorite dresses, as her grandmother had made it the month before she'd moved to the mainland to live with Stacey's brother.

A fierce wave of missing dove through her, and her mouth turned downward. She understood why NeNe couldn't stay here after the death of her husband, especially when he'd left the estate to Stacey.

They'd talked about her plans while NeNe sewed, while NeNe braided her hair, while Stacey wept because she felt like she was losing both of her grandparents within a couple of months. She'd leaned heavily on her boyfriend at the time, Randy. They'd dated for years, and she even had a shiny diamond on her finger when she came home one day to find a note on her kitchen counter.

A note.

A letter goodbye, actually, with no forwarding address. His place had been cleaned out, and Stacey didn't have the funds or inclination to track him down. It was the first time she'd been ghosted, and she didn't want to experience a second time.

Surprisingly, that wasn't when she'd sworn off men. "Should've been," she said to her reflection. With a jolt of realization, she said, "You're doing it again."

Her suite phone shrilled out the old-school tone, blasting her from this dark space inside her mind. She yanked her eyes from herself and lifted the receiver. "Stacey."

"Fisher DuPont has just arrived. Should I send him down the hall?"

"No," Stacey practically barked. "No, thank you, Tayla. I'll meet him in the lobby in a couple of minutes."

"I'll let him know." Tayla hung up, and Stacey returned to the mirror.

Am I doing it again? she wondered. Fisher didn't seem like the kind of man who could disappear into thin air. After all, his hotel was here, and surely he had to be physically present to conduct some business.

But with his money...he could definitely fly the coop whenever he wanted. And he had unlimited resources and ways to communicate. He could certainly make conference calls or video in for a meeting from anywhere in the world.

Stacey was tired of the yo-yo she'd been tied to since yesterday morning. She liked Fisher, and it was just lunch. Maybe she could dig for insider information during the appetizers.

She gave her hair one more fluff and left her suite. One date wasn't dangerous to her heart health. She could go on one date.

She pushed into the lobby, stunned into slowing her steps at the pure handsomeness of the man waiting there for her. He wore a bright blue T-shirt with a black suit jacket over it, with a pair of jeans. He made casual look sophisticated and sexy. No one else would be able to pair that jacket with a T-shirt and get away with it, but he made it look like everyone on Wall Street was dressing this way.

He offered her his right arm from all the way across the room, and Stacey felt a gravitational pull toward him. Relief that he'd offered his right arm flowed through her. Then he wouldn't feel her crooked pinky if they ended up holding hands on the way to the car.

"Hey," he said, his face breaking into a wide smile. "For a second there, I thought you wouldn't come out."

Stacey laughed, because it was the natural thing to do— and he didn't know how close to home he'd just hit. "For a minute there, I almost didn't." She crossed the room and linked her hand through his arm. A ping of electricity traveled up her arm into her shoulder and the warmth from his body seeped into hers.

She could do this. Be herself. Enjoy herself. She didn't have to marry him. Or even go on a second date.

"Where are we going?" she asked.

"I thought we'd try The Hulas," he said.

"Ah, the historic district."

"Have you been?"

"I grew up on the island," Stacey said. "I've been. I love their seafood platter, but I think they only serve that for dinner."

He tightened his arm, tucking her hand right against his hard side. "A reason to go back, then."

EIGHT

FISHER WAS sure he'd hallucinated this whole thing. So when Stacey emerged from the depths of her bed and breakfast wearing a stunning floral dress, he hadn't quite known how to react. He hadn't said she looked nice, or given her a compliment at all.

"I like the dress," he said as they walked toward his car.

"Thanks. My NeNe made it."

"NeNe?"

"My grandmother." She stopped a few paces from the red sports car. "Good thing I didn't spend too long on my hair."

Fisher wanted to run his fingers through the strands, find out if it was as silky as it looked. He kept his right hand in his pocket and his left glued to his side. "I'll drive slow."

She tossed her hair and gathered it into a loose ponytail. "It's fine. There's no better way to get around the island than in a convertible."

"Do you have one?"

"Heavens, no," she said. "But my—" She cut off as if someone had pressed mute on her vocal chords. She pressed her lips together and shook her head. "No."

Fisher hadn't expected her to spill her life history on the first date, but a prick of disappointment stung his lungs. He let her retreat while he opened the door for her, and watched as she gracefully sank into the seat.

He liked her too much already, and he wasn't even sure why. Maybe because she hadn't fawned over the mere sight of him. Maybe because she was a smart and savvy business-woman who kept her finger on the pulse of her competitors. He'd always admired women who knew what they wanted and went after it.

"My mother and step-father live in Michigan," he said when he got behind the wheel. "I don't know how you've grown up with all this humidity. When I first landed here, it was like I got hit with a wall of water."

She smiled and leaned her elbow on the windowsill of the car. "Is that where you grew up? Michigan?"

"Ann Arbor." He flashed her a smile. "It's a great place. I think you'd like it." He let out a slow breath. "The trees in the fall...they're something to behold."

"Fall," Stacey repeated. "I don't think we have that season here."

Fisher chuckled and agreed. "Not that I've seen." He kept in contact with his mom and step-dad, but he hadn't been to visit in months. "I'm going in October," he said, making the decision on the spot.

"Sounds nice."

There was no way he could invite her to travel with him, so he just smiled and managed to keep the car on the road despite his nerves. He couldn't believe how anxious he'd been leading up to this lunch. He'd attended much more stressful dinners and events than this, and yet the merger of a multi-million dollar company didn't seem hard at all when compared to talking to the beautiful Stacey Stapleton.

"Tell me about your parents," she said. "What's your step-dad's name?"

"Denver DuPont. He sold insurance for forty years."

"Wow. I can't imagine doing anything for forty years."

"Not even run your B&B?"

"Well…I guess that."

"So you like your job?"

She glanced at him, her striking green eyes reminding him that just because he had billions of dollars didn't mean he was worthy of her. "Yeah, I really like running Aloha Hideaway."

"I can tell." He pulled into the parking lot at The Hulas, the cars everywhere not exactly comforting. A bus pulled up several yards down the road and people piled off of it, all of them heading straight for the restaurant. "Maybe I should've gotten a reservation."

"Nah, they're fast," she said. "And they'll bring around the most delicious crab toast, with the *tiniest* slivers of avocado you've ever had. It's worth showing up at the busiest times just for that."

"Noted." Fisher relaxed as they moved into the restaurant. Stacey seemed to like him, and the conversation hadn't been pressed or awkward on the way over. Sure, he hadn't been out with anyone in a while, but it felt a little like riding a bicycle.

He gave his name to the hostess, and she flashed him a bright smile and said, "Fifteen minutes okay?"

"Just fine," Stacey said, pressing in close to him with a smile the size of the bay. She tugged him away from the hostess station to a tiny patch of bench, where they somehow squeezed themselves into the space.

"Siblings?" he asked, starting with the basics. He soaked in the closeness of her. So close he could see the freckles splattered across her nose and cheeks that she'd tried to cover up with makeup.

"One younger brother. Scott." She nodded like his name summed up everything. "He moved to California, oh, it's got to be about fifteen years ago now." The smile that ran across her face looked a bit pinched along the edges.

"You miss him." He wasn't asking. Fisher had plenty of experience dealing with people and most of them weren't great at hiding their emotions. Stacey was better than most, but he could still hear the emotion in her voice.

"My parents are still here," she said, brightening. "They lead tours over in the volcanic national park."

"You see them often?"

"Often enough." She twisted toward him. "What about you? You can't be the only son in the Davenport Development Group."

Fisher laughed, but the sound held little mirth. "I assure you I am."

"So no siblings?"

He regarded her, contemplating how much to trust her

with. Anything he said wouldn't be something she could find on the Internet. In fact, if it was, she'd probably already know.

"I have two half-sisters," he said. "My parents split up when I was four, and my mom remarried, and she and Denver had two girls. Lily and Kyla."

"And they're all in Michigan."

"Yes, ma'am."

She squinted, her expression turning darker. Her bright green eyes actually took on a hue of hazel. "Do you like me, Fisher?"

Stunned by the bluntness of her question, all Fisher could do was nod.

"Then you'll never call me *ma'am* again. I'm not even forty yet." She added a playful smile to the end of the sentence, and Fisher didn't have time to answer or confirm before his name was called for the next table.

———

The following morning, Fisher's feet pounded the hard-packed sand about a mile from Sweet Breeze. For some reason, he couldn't run fast enough today. His chest heaved, and he knew he'd have to slow down soon. He couldn't keep up this pace, not after filling himself with the best seafood Hawaii had to offer the day before.

The conversation at lunch had been everything Fisher had hoped for. Stacey had only clammed up that one time, right before she got in the convertible, and she'd told him about how she'd inherited Aloha Hideaway from her grandfather after his death, and how her grandmother had moved to the mainland to live with her brother. He'd learned why her face turned sad at the mention of her grandparents, as she'd lived with them during some "important times" of her life.

She hadn't elaborated on what those times were, but Fisher reasoned there was time to find out. He'd dropped her off at her bed and breakfast without asking her out again, but there'd been a fantastic hug. He could still feel the form of her pressed against him, smell the floral scent of her gardens on her skin, and see the rejection of his next date invitation.

He'd texted. Maybe that had been the problem. Maybe she wanted him to ask her out in person or call. But his pride hadn't allowed him to do that. Yet.

He was still reeling from her *I had a great time, but I think we should leave it at that.*

Leave it at that?

The words pushed him to run faster, harder, longer. Eventually, his body couldn't go anymore and he slowed to a stop, his whole upper half heaving as he sought oxygen. The sun was hot for only eight o'clock in the morning, and the humidity wasn't helping with the required quota of air he needed. It felt like he was trying to inhale soup, and he wondered when his body would acclimate to this tropical climate.

He straightened and tipped his head back, letting the warmth and light from the sun bathe his face. He was miles from his suite, and he wasn't sure he could get back on his own. He definitely couldn't make it back without something to drink and probably a whole lot of carbs. Thankfully, Hawaii had enough food stands along the beach to get his system back in symbiosis and he stepped up to one that had smoke coming out of the roof and the longest line in front of it.

"Spam and egg burrito," he said when it was his turn to order. "Two of 'em. And as much water as I can get." He shoved a fifty dollar bill across the counter, the only denomination he carried when running. He'd learned that twenty sometimes wasn't enough and one hundred could get him mugged in the wrong neighborhood—at least in LA.

The man delivered the food in record time, and Fisher said, "Keep the change," as he walked away. He unwrapped one foil-covered burrito and devoured it in record time. Bit by bit, his strength came back.

As much as he didn't want to admit it, he needed help with Stacey. He didn't want to mention anything to Marshall, as the man would remind him of why they didn't date. The island was a small space, almost a closed society, at least among locals. And neither of them were interested in the fling a tourist would provide. Fisher had too many zeroes in his bank account to deal with that headache.

Fisher found a spot of sand and sat down to enjoy his second burrito a little more slowly. He loved Hawaii, the weather notwithstanding. He realized most people loved the weather here, and he decided he could too.

His phone buzzed against his bicep, but he ignored it. The pocket was too darn small to get the device in and out, and it would take an act of God to get him to answer a call right now.

Maybe it's Stacey...

The thought infiltrated his mind and wouldn't let go.

It isn't Stacey. It's Owen.

The mental battle begun, and in the end, Fisher did not pull out his phone to check. Stacey didn't seem like the waffling type, and she'd turned him down less than twelve hours ago. She hadn't acted strangely on their date, and—he got up and brushed the sand from his shorts.

"You're going to drive yourself insane," he muttered. "Gotta stop thinking about it." He opted to take the paved path back to the hotel, completely ignoring his own advice. He simply couldn't figure out where he'd gone wrong, what he'd said to make her think one date was enough, or why she wouldn't be interested in a second outing with him.

As he arrived back at Sweet Breeze and entered his private elevator, he did two things. One, he checked his text. Yep, just something about a meeting from Owen.

Two, he determined he'd have to go see Stacey face-to-face to find out what was going on to make her say no to a second date when all indicators had shown that she'd enjoyed their first.

NINE

"MAMA, DAD." Stacey stepped through the back door of her parent's house and into their oasis of a backyard. Sure enough, her dad looked up from the roasting pit, where he knelt, working to pull the meat up from the chambers carved into the earth.

"Stacey." Her mom wiped her hands on her apron and gave Stacey a hug. "How's Aloha Hideaway?" She pushed her own red hair now streaked with gray away from her face.

"Busy." Stacey pushed out a sigh. "We've got a full turnover today."

"Good thing Dad made so much food."

"I'll take whatever you'll let me." Stacey smiled at her approaching father and embraced him too. "Smells amazing, Dad."

"Aloha, Stacia." Her father always spoke with a Spanish-Hawaiian accent, and while Stacey hadn't inherited hardly any of his native genes, she felt a deep connection to her dad, the same way she had with her grandparents.

"Its days like this when I miss the food truck." Stacey stepped away from her father and tucked her hands in her back pockets. It was like her memory dams had flooded these past few days, and she let the years she'd spent growing up in the narrow galley kitchen in the truck wash over her.

She'd learned old family recipes in that food truck kitchen, as well as several from time spent in a real kitchen with her NeNe. She didn't spend much time cooking now, but the ingredients and proportions were still there in her mind. She still loved grilled pineapple, especially when it was freshly picked from the plantations that lined her parent's property. She loved ahi on the rare side, and she had never put anything in her mouth that her father had made that didn't make her want to die and go to heaven.

"What did you put in the imu today?" she asked.

"Chicken, turkey, plantains, sweet potatoes." He smiled at her and returned to the underground oven to collect the food. He'd made enough to feed an entire luau of people, but Stacey said nothing. She'd take all the leftovers back to her weekly staff meeting, and everyone would be happy.

"Tell us what's new this week," her father said, something he requested every week.

The image of Fisher's finely sculpted face flashed through Stacey's mind. She could still smell the masculine scent of his cologne, along with the salt on his skin. Still feel the gentle pressure of his embrace when he'd dropped her off and could still see him slide effortlessly into the convertible that practically sat on the ground before he drove off.

"Nothing," she said, her voice betraying her the slightest bit. If her mama or dad noticed, they didn't say. "Same old happenings at Aloha Hideaway. There's a storm coming in. Got a notice from the Weather Service and everything."

"We got it at the park too," Mama said. "James isn't concerned."

"They said the winds could be up to sixty miles per hour." Stacey piled a soft piece of sweet potato on a browned length of chicken and put the whole thing in her mouth. The traditional ti leaves gave everything such beautiful flavor, and the potatoes, despite being cooked for hours, had great consistency against the chicken.

"He says we get reports like that all the time." Mama shrugged.

Stacey didn't get them, and she'd decided to take the warning seriously. She had her maintenance crew boarding the windows on Monday night—or she would once they had their staff meeting that afternoon.

"So you'll be working on Tuesday?" Stacey managed to keep the alarm out of her voice.

"Probably."

She didn't understand why she was the only one taking this storm warning seriously. She'd mentioned it to Fisher, who hadn't seemed to know about the report at all. She supposed he had people who had people to take care of such things. She wasn't even sure how he could board up all those windows, and the open-air pools on the very top floors had no protection at all.

While Getaway Bay was somewhat sheltered by the long arm of land on the south side, the surf could still be disastrous with a true tropical storm and with winds as high as the report suggested they'd be.

So she'd board her windows and made sure her generators had fuel and that her contingency plans for her guests were in place. She didn't want to be left high and dry—or low and wet—just because no one else took the report seriously.

"So," her mom said. "Are you seeing anyone?"

Stacey would've normally groaned and rolled her eyes. Her parents knew everything that had happened and Mama had been the one to suggest a break from the single male population. She'd obviously changed her mind.

"Not anything too serious," she said. "But there is someone."

Mama smiled as she set the last of the silverware on the table. "Good. I'd like a grandbaby or two."

"You have a grandbaby or two," she said. "Remember how Scott has three kids in California?" Stacey cocked her eyebrows at her mom as a fierce longing for children of her own swept through her.

She'd managed to keep the thoughts of becoming a mother far behind the closed doors around her heart. But with the recent addition of Fisher to her life, everything felt like it had been blown wide open.

By the time she returned to Aloha Hideaway, most of the staff was waiting in one of the break rooms in the east wing where they met every week. "There's more in the car," she said, setting the large aluminum foil baking pan full of chicken on the table. "Tayla, grab the plates and silverware. Betty, Dillan, you guys come help me with the rest of the food." She smiled around at her housekeepers, her groundskeepers, her friends. "We'll be right back."

With everyone eating and laughing, Stacey glanced around and felt right at home. Comfortable. Complete.

Again, Fisher snuck into her mind. Had she felt more complete when eating fish tacos across from him? Possibly. Maybe not. She didn't really know.

Which was why she didn't need him complicating her already great life. Because that was what men like Fisher DuPont did. They complicated things.

And Stacey didn't need that.

"All right," she said once most of the plates were clear and the chatter had increased. The voices quieted and the last conversation between Lizzie and Honor, the housekeepers, died.

"Life updates," she said. "Let's start with Marge."

They went around the table, each of them taking a minute to talk about their dogs, or their parents, or a significant other. When it was Stacey's turn, she said, "Henry has finally started to share his chew toys with Hugs, so I'm counting that as my weekly win." She smiled around at the group. She often shared about her schnauzers, so her update wasn't out of the ordinary. But she knew it absolutely wasn't her biggest win of the week.

That could've been her newfound knowledge of the tourism management meeting, or that she'd learned a few things about Sweet Breeze during her stay. But it wasn't

either of those things. It was the date with Fisher that still
had her too warm and left wanting for another date.

But she wasn't stupid, and her heart still had cracks in it.
She'd thought they'd healed, but every minute she'd spent
with Fisher had testified to her that they hadn't. Because she
was so willing to let him in, laugh with him, let him hold her
hand.

She wished. There hadn't been any hand-holding, much
to her disappointment.

"Stace?" Betty's hand landed on Stacey's forearm, and
she jolted out of yesterday afternoon's dream date.

"Oh, yeah." She scanned the people at the table. "Sorry.
Let's start with the storm."

"No," Betty said quietly, leaning closer. Stacey looked at
her and found her eyes riveted on the doorway. She nodded
in that direction. "You have a visitor."

Stacey followed Betty's gaze and found Fisher standing
in the doorway, halfway in the room and halfway out as if he
couldn't commit to coming all the way in. Two sides of her
battled, and she wasn't sure if she should be excited at his
presence or absolutely furious.

She marched forward, Tropical Storm Stacey, and Fisher
seemed to get that weather warning, because he backed into
the hall and all the way out to the lobby.

"I just wanted to talk to you for a second." He ducked his
head in that adorable way he had, which only seemed to fuel
the cyclone in Stacey's chest. In a good way? She wasn't sure
cyclones could ever be considered good.

"I have a phone," she said. "And how did you get in here
anyway?"

"The front door's unlocked," he said. "I rang the bell." He indicated the silver apparatus on the front desk. "No one came, and I heard laughter, and I...followed it."

"You interrupted my staff meeting."

Fisher looked impressed, like he didn't expect her five-room bed and breakfast to hold staff meetings. "I'm sorry."

Stacey cocked her hip and folded her arms, trying to calm down a little. She didn't need word of her tirade getting out to the guests, and any of them could walk through the lobby at any time. "What do you want to say?"

He opened his mouth and snapped it shut again.

"I—"

"I know you want to go out with me again," he said over her. "I know you had a good time at lunch yesterday. What I don't know is why you said no to a second date."

Stacey wasn't one hundred percent sure either, and it was so, so hard to speak to him about this to his face. She'd been half disappointed when he hadn't asked her out again when he'd dropped her off yesterday and half relieved. Then that blasted text had come, and it had been much easier to say no when she didn't have to look into those brilliant blue eyes.

Emotions stormed in her chest, and she didn't know how to release them. Her heart couldn't hold them, so she looked away and pushed the breath out of her body, willing the tumult inside her to go with it.

Only partially calm—a state she was starting to associate with being in Fisher's presence—she said, "I...I can't." That was as eloquent as she could get at the moment.

"You can't go out with me?"

"Right."

"Why not?"

She saw two sides of him with those two words. The powerful, defiant billionaire, and the vulnerable, boyish man who just wanted a second date.

"I don't trust you," she said.

"All right." He took a step forward, somehow able to sense that the storm inside her had blown itself almost all the way out. "I can earn trust, if you give me time." Those eyes blazed, and Stacey couldn't help the attraction between them.

"I'm scared," she said.

"And you can tell me why on our next date," he said, taking another step toward her. "We've all got a past, Stacey. Mine's not exactly roses and sunshine. And I can tell you about it on our next date."

Stacey wanted to go out with him. She had last night when she'd said no. "When do you want to go out?"

"Right now."

TEN

FISHER SAW THE INDECISION, the desire, the desperation on Stacey's face. A couple of those he didn't like, but he didn't give her an inch. If she told him no for a second time, he'd go. Lick his wounds and figure out what he'd done wrong. But he wouldn't come begging for a third time.

Fisher had learned over the years that some things were worth fighting for, and while he'd never thought he'd credit his father for much of anything, he had to give him that. It had been his mother who'd taught him to hold his tongue, wait when he wanted to speak, listen when he wanted to prove he was right.

He knew absolutely that Stacey wanted to go out with him again.

"I'm in the middle of my staff meeting," she said.

Fisher stepped over to the leather couch, hoping it was half as comfortable as it looked. "I'll wait." He sank onto the furniture, satisfied at the plushness of the cushions.

A pretty pinch appeared between her eyes, but she gave him a curt nod and spun around, disappearing through the door that had been slightly ajar when he'd arrived. It shut firmly this time, and he couldn't hear anything from that wing of the house.

He'd seen a couple of empty rooms before happening upon the meeting, and he wondered why Stacey didn't sell those too. She could obviously get the bookings, and his curiosity burned through him, urging him to get up and explore Aloha Hideaway.

He didn't move a muscle, though. He'd gotten the heated vibe from Stacey just by walking down the hall and positioning himself in the doorway. He could imagine how she might go volcanic if she found him snooping around.

Don't need to do that, he told himself, willing the seconds to tick by faster.

She'd finish her meeting and they'd go out, and Fisher could ask her about that wing of the house then.

Relaxing into the cushions, he attempted to look casual on the outside. But inside, his heartbeat kept tripping over itself and his mind raced like it was trying to win a NASCAR title.

He wouldn't ask her about that wing of the house either. He'd tell her about his past and hope she opened up to him a little bit. But he wouldn't push her. Showing up here unannounced had already been a mighty shove and he was sure he was walking on thin ice as it was.

What felt like forever later, but was really only about forty-five minutes, the door opened. Fisher couldn't help how his attention whipped to it, only to find Tayla, the bright, bubbly, blonde smiling in his direction.

"She'll be out in a minute."

Fisher returned the grin and kept himself from jumping to his feet. Another ten minutes passed with Tayla pretending to work at the counter before Stacey appeared.

She'd changed into a denim jumper that made his mouth dry. A navy blouse complemented her hair and made her eyes pop. Or maybe that was the fireworks ricocheting between them.

Fisher rose slowly, not really trusting himself not to rush her, sweep her into his arms, and kiss her. And wow, it had been a while since he'd kissed a woman.

"You look great," he said. "Ready?"

"I wasn't really sure what the occasion was," she said, casting a nervous glance at Tayla, who didn't look away from her computer. No matter what was on the screen, it couldn't have been more interesting than this exchange, so Fisher gave the woman credit for her professionalism.

"Maybe we'll just take a walk." He extended his left hand, an invitation for Stacey to come, hold hands with him, go, walk, be together.

She stared at his fingers like they were individual cobras, and then sidled over to his other side, slipping her left hand into his right. "I, um, I broke my pinky a few years back and my other hand is all deformed."

Fisher could barely make sense of her words. First off, his brain was firing all kinds of messages around his body. Things like, *Wow, her skin is soft*, and *I really like holding hands with her*, and *Deformed?*

He spoke the last word and followed it with, "I don't believe that."

Stacey held up her right hand and twisted it so he could see her pinky. "Look how it's all bent."

She'd definitely broken it—badly—in the past. But deformed? "It's a little crooked," he said. "I wouldn't call that deformed." Just because he could, he reached up with his free hand and touched her pinky finger. She flinched as if he'd shocked her, and Fisher's eyes locked onto hers.

"Looks about perfect," he said, his voice a throaty hum he had no idea how he'd achieved. The last woman who'd made him feel like this…. He'd never met a woman that made him feel like this. Soft. Warm. But strong. Powerful.

The electricity between them crackled, and Fisher thought it best to get away from Tayla before they sent lightning down on her. Once free of the Aloha Hideaway lobby, he took a deep breath and promptly changed his mind.

He'd seen and smelled the food in the conference room where he'd found Stacey, so he couldn't suggest dinner. But he didn't want to walk through the humidity either, though he'd do almost anything to keep Stacey's hand in his.

"Maybe you'd like to see the aquarium at Sweet Breeze," he said. "Or did you scope that out while you were staying with us?"

"There's an aquarium in your hotel?"

"On the sixth floor," he said. "We have a small garden too. Nothing like yours," he added quickly.

"What happened to just walking?"

He glanced at her, wondering if she'd laugh at him if he told her the truth. "I can't stand the humidity here," he admitted as he approached his car. "I feel like I'm swimming all the time, and I can't get a proper breath."

Stacey tossed her cute curls and grinned at him. "You'll acclimate."

"That's what people keep telling me, but I've lived here for five years, and I gotta say, it's not any better than when I stepped off the plane the first time."

"You've been here for five years?"

"Yes." He opened her door and waited for her to get in. In shorts that short, he wondered how she'd even do it.

With grace, as he found out when she sank onto his leather seats. "But Sweet Breeze has only been open for ten months."

Fisher closed her door and rounded the front of the car before settling into the driver's seat. "I oversaw everything from concept to completion," he said. "And I couldn't do it from somewhere else."

She regarded him with a curious glint in her eyes, but she didn't say anything. He drove back to Sweet Breeze, only a few minutes away, and pulled up to the valet. Sterling exchanged pleasantries with him and Fisher took Stacey's hand in his again as they entered the hotel.

"We broke ground over three years ago," Fisher said. "I came every day, even swung a hammer a few times."

"I don't believe that." Stacey's voice could only be categorized as flirtatious.

"Believe it, missy. These muscles are good for more than just show." He laughed, the action freeing him in a way he hadn't experienced in a long time. He led her to the event elevators, where they joined a group of tourists who got off on the fourth floor to go to the movie theater.

Fisher pushed six and the doors sealed him and Stacey inside. Alone. Anxiety pounded through his bloodstream, and he squeezed her fingers a little tighter.

"Nervous?" she asked.

"Is it that obvious?"

"My nene—grandmother—could sense energy in people," Stacey said with a small shrug. "She taught me a few things."

Fisher swallowed and nodded. "I'm a bit nervous."

"About what?"

Being alone with you sounded weird.

Kissing you sounded too forward.

Hoping you don't reject me again sounded desperate.

In the end, Fisher decided to go with the truth again. "I like you, Stacey. And you've already turned me down, so I'm trying to figure out what I did wrong the first time and make sure I don't do it again."

The elevator dinged and the doors slid open. Neither of them moved.

"You didn't do anything wrong." Her green eyes were endless, and Fisher imagined himself in the middle of the densest tropical forest in the world. That was the color of her eyes, the fresh scent of her hair, the magic in her touch.

"I haven't been out with a woman in a long time," he said.

"I haven't been out with a man in four years," she said. "Can you beat that?"

"You're the first woman I've dated in Hawaii."

She smiled and reached up with her free hand to run her fingers down the side of his face. The gesture was sweet, something his mother would do when she was proud of him. But it was also charged too, filled with unspoken promises of kissing later, and Fisher leaned into the touch to give his consent to such thoughts.

"So you win," she said with that flirtatious smile. "Which means you get to tell me your story first."

"I was going to anyway. Maybe the loser should start."

She giggled and flung her arm out to catch the elevator doors as they started to slide closed. "Nice try." She stepped off the elevator and he followed her.

Fisher exhaled like he was put out. "Fine. There was this woman in Los Angeles." He hadn't thought about Juliana in a long time. "She worked for my father, which should've been my first clue that we wouldn't get along."

"You don't like your father much, do you?"

"No." Fisher paused at the entrance to the aquarium. A man stood there to welcome people, but no tickets were required. His face brightened when he saw Fisher.

"Mister DuPont, welcome to the aquarium today." His eyes flickered to Stacey and his whole face turned white. "Stacey?" Her name was nothing more than a squeak.

"Oh, hi, Kai," she said, the rhyme sounding funny coming from her mouth. "I didn't know you worked here."

Kai nodded, his head full of dark hair swinging with the movement.

"Of course, I didn't even know there was an aquarium here until ten minutes ago."

"Fifteen, at least," Fisher said. "We talked to the valet for a few minutes."

Stacey rolled her eyes, but it was a playful gesture, and Fisher found himself enjoying this flirtation game more than he ever had. "Fine, fifteen minutes." She tucked her hair behind her ear and smiled at Kai. "Good to see you."

Fisher watched the other man's face turn the color of tomatoes, but he said nothing as he entered the aquarium too. When they were safely away from Kai, he leaned down and said, "So he has a crush on you."

Stacey paused—froze, really—and whispered, "He does not."

Fisher cast him a glance and found him staring after them. "He sure does. And he's still watching you."

"Maybe it's you he's concerned about," she hissed back, still unmoving. "I mean, you're his boss and everything."

"I come here all the time," Fisher said. "It's not me." He nudged Stacey to move forward and she did, though it seemed like her legs were made of wood.

"I've known him for ages. We practically grew up together."

"Dang," Fisher said. "Now I feel bad for the guy." He tugged Stacey a little closer, glad she hadn't had feelings for Kai.

"You didn't finish telling me about your last girlfriend."

Fisher yawned as if the whole conversation were quite boring. "Juliana thought I could help her get ahead. When she learned how different from my father I am, she broke up with me." His eyebrows bent into a V. "Too bad neither of us figured that out before I'd bought a ring and proposed."

Stacey sucked in a breath and stepped in front of him.

"You're blocking my view of the Japanese angelfish," he said.

She didn't move. Didn't blink. "You were engaged?"

"Yes." He put on his calm mask, the one that wouldn't reveal how much it had cost him to ask Juliana to marry him only to have her leave him when she quit her job, keep the diamond ring, and start dating another powerful executive very soon after all of that had happened. He didn't care about the money, but he wasn't sure he had all the pieces of his heart back in place yet. Or his ego.

"Did you get married?"

"No."

Stacey tilted her head to the side. "Did you require your fiancée to sign a pre-nuptial agreement?"

"Yes." He wasn't sure if she appreciated this or not. But Fisher hadn't worked for his wealth only to lose it to someone like Juliana. Looking at Stacey, he knew with certainty that she wasn't anything like Juliana. Not even close.

She was beautiful. She was smart. She was driven. But she wasn't looking to ride Fisher's coattails to glory.

She did stay in your hotel, a voice whispered in his mind. But it was silenced easily when Stacey tipped up onto her toes and brushed her lips against his cheek. Her touch was there and then gone, light and heavy at the same time. She returned to his side, sighing as she leaned into him and brought her free hand to his forearm. "The Japanese angelfish is stunning, isn't it?"

ELEVEN

STACEY'S CONCENTRATION waffled from the bright yellow fish in front of her to the handsome man next to her. If she were being honest, it wasn't an even split, and the fish weren't winning.

Fisher had been right; the aquarium wasn't very large. But it did have an impressive number of fish, and everything was obviously state of the art. No matter what, it was one aquarium more than Stacey had at Aloha Hideaway.

They stepped past Kai for the second time, and Stacey could barely look at him. Did he really have a crush on her? And for how long?

Doesn't matter, she told herself. It was obvious to anyone who glanced their way that she was out on a date with Fisher. Now, whether they were dat*ing* or not, she wasn't sure, even though he'd used that word.

Did two dates qualify as dating? She'd been out of the pond for so long, she wasn't sure. She was sure that her rapid pulse was likely to induce a heart attack, and she was sure that his cologne had to be made of some illegal substance that simply smelled too good.

"I know you were eating when I stopped by," he said. "But might you be interested in dinner? We have a few restaurants here on site, or I could have the kitchen send us something to any of the pools...."

"How many pools do you have?" Stacey hadn't worn her swimming suit, but then again, one didn't need a suit to sit by the pool with a dreamy man and eat something fried.

"Eight public pools," he said. "For guests."

"And you?"

"Just the one."

She glanced up as if she could see through the layers of steel, glass, and cement. "And which floor is yours?"

"I'm on twenty-eight," he said.

"Do you share?"

"Share what? The floor?" He seemed genuinely shocked.

Stacey couldn't believe he had an entire floor of this place to himself. And she'd felt bad about keeping the east wing separate from the guests.

"It's smaller than the others," he said, his face taking on a delicious ruddiness that was dangerous to Stacey's heart health.

"What? The twenty-eighth floor?"

"Yes. The building tapers up to accommodate the open-air pools."

Stacey really enjoyed teasing him, and she skipped ahead of him and turned around to walk backward. "Oh, so it's only ten thousand square feet instead of fifteen?"

He caught her mocking tone and smiled as he shook his head. He really was adorable, and Stacey couldn't help thinking that he was the most down-to-earth billionaire she'd ever met. Fine, he was the *only* billionaire she'd ever met. She hadn't been prepared to like him, this man who'd shown up in her bay and built this towering hotel she'd vowed to hate for life.

Problem was, she didn't hate it. And she didn't dislike Fisher. Quite the opposite on both points, actually.

"Would you like to see my suite?" he asked, still advancing toward her.

Oh, she would. She also felt it a little too...personal. And dangerous. Before she could figure out how to answer in a way that would come across as a rejection, his eyes widened.

"Stace—"

Her back hit something hard and she stumbled, searching for a way to keep her feet under her. *Please, no*, she thought right before she felt herself falling.

Then both of Fisher's hands landed on her body, creating burning patches of skin against skin. "Whoa. I got you."

Stacey stayed rigid, but at least she managed to grab onto his shoulders. And wow, he totally had muscles that were for more than just show, though the show part was pretty fantastic too.

Time froze, with her bent backward and Fisher holding her as if he'd bent her to kiss her. Her eyes traveled to his mouth, and she wondered what it would be like to taste that little smirk, draw it off his face until he wasn't giving her that sexy half-grin but kissing her back without his usual careful, controlled demeanor.

Fisher thawed first, and he set her on her feet and let his hands fall to his sides. "Gotta be careful," he said, clearing his throat and falling back a couple of feet. "We have some killer plants around here."

Stacey stared at him for a moment past comfortable, straightened, and fluffed her hair. "I'm fine. Thank you." She turned and glared at the giant potted plant that had almost made her fall in front of Fisher for the second time. She harrumphed and turned back to Fisher to find he'd closed the distance between them.

"Oh." She squeaked as he took her into his arms. The movement was effortless, and she fit right against his chest.

"So not my place," he said, his voice a pleasant hum in her ear. "Did you go up to the rooftop pool when you were here? I'll have food sent up."

She was sure he could have anything he wanted—her included—and that sent a shiver of fear mingling with the current of electricity already racing up and down her spine.

"All right," she heard herself say. "I want fried calamari and something with a lot of cheese."

"Calamari and something cheesy. I think we can do that." He stepped away from her and took her hand before strolling toward the elevator. Back on the main floor, he stepped over to the front desk and spoke to the concierge, who was made of all smiles and nods.

Stacey stood in the midst of the busyness of the hotel, so different from Aloha Hideaway and yet so vibrant. She realized Fisher was the same way—a man so different from others Stacey knew, and yet so vibrant. But just like Sweet Breeze was in a class of its own and there was no way Aloha

Hideaway could compete, Stacey felt like Fisher was way out of her league.

————

Half an hour later, the wind pulled and pushed Stacey's hair as she lifted another piece of cheesy garlic bread to her mouth. "This stuff is *amazing*." The toast crunched against her teeth and while she'd cared the first time, now she didn't.

Fisher tipped his head back as he drained the last of his soda. "I'm glad you like it." He sat close enough to convey the message that they were more than friends—or that he wanted to be—but he hadn't made a move yet.

"So did you want to tell me why you don't trust me and what you're afraid of?"

She almost choked on the last bite of her bread. He handed her the can of Diet Coke she'd requested and she gulped it, the burn of carbonation welcome in her suddenly dry throat.

"It's not really you," she said.

He waited for her to continue, and Stacey found she wanted to tell him the truth, trust him with part of herself. But wasn't that what always got her in trouble?

"I was engaged too." She cleared her throat. "Twice, actually."

Fisher, who normally gave no reaction at all, coughed and lifted his eyebrows. "Twice?"

Stacey focused on the pool deck, the bay breeze no longer quite so friendly. "I lost three years of my life wearing a diamond ring. If I were to ever get serious with someone again, I'd just want to elope. Run away and get married one weekend, no engagement." As she spoke, she realized that was exactly what she wanted. She would not wear another ring from a man who could walk out of her life whenever he wanted.

"What happened?" He threaded his fingers through hers, stroking his pinky down her crooked one.

"I still have one of the rings. My boyfriend—fiancé—whatever—Randy, he left one day. Just gone. No forwarding address. No email. Nothing. Well, I got a note. It was stupid." She could still see the words in his slanted handwriting, still feel the way her stomach had swooped and sloshed.

He squeezed her hand and she said, "So I still have that ring. I should sell it or something. Put new carpet in my guest rooms." Why she hadn't thought of that until now, she wasn't sure. She exhaled. "Anyway, the second time I was engaged, it was going on two years and we still hadn't set a date—which made a lot of sense when I found out he had another girlfriend on Lanai."

Fisher hissed his breath out between his teeth. "You're kidding."

"Not even a little bit." She looked up and met his blue-eyed gaze. His expression held compassion, sympathy, kindness. "So I swore off men four years ago and I've been focused on Aloha Hideaway."

Fisher nodded like her choices made a lot of sense. To Stacey, it had been pure self-preservation.

"I'm not going anywhere," he said. "And I'm not dating anyone on Lanai."

"Good to know." She smiled at him and it felt like it would be easy, natural, to lean closer to him and maybe he'd lift his arm around her shoulders and then she'd slide further into his chest and they'd watch the sun set over Getaway Bay in the comfort of each other's arms.

So she did exactly that, and Fisher did precisely what she'd fantasized, and the sun drifted toward the horizon with that sense of peace Stacey had been craving.

"We should get you back," he said as dusk settled over the water, making it appear more black than blue.

"Yeah." She exhaled as she untangled herself from his arms and swung her legs over the edge of the couch. "What are you doing about the weather warning?"

"Weather warning?" He looked at her with a blip of confusion in those eyes. "Oh, right. My GM will take care of it."

"Well, at Aloha Hideaway, I'm the GM." She gave him a flirty smile and smoothed her shorts down. They descended in the pool elevator, which smelled like chlorine and wet hair, and he drove her back to her bed and breakfast.

He met her at the passenger door, but he didn't step toward the doors of Aloha Hideaway. "So when can I see you again?" he asked.

Stacey wanted to see him the very next day, but she didn't want to be too forward. Or maybe she did. She'd never felt like she'd been on such a teeter-totter before. Up, down. Left, right. Coming, going.

"When are you available?"

"Whenever you are." He put one hand on the top of the car, keeping her between it and his body.

Stacey looked up at him and felt herself falling. *Up, then down.*

She put one hand on his waist and let it drift around to his back while the other reached up to cradle his face. He growled, a deep, guttural noise that made Stacey move a little slower just to tease him a little longer.

She tipped up on her toes, glad when he took her into his arms, because she was definitely going to fall as soon as her lips touched his.

Her eyes drifted closed. She pulled in a breath, waiting for him to bridge the last remaining gap between them. When he finally did, a sigh passed through her whole body. His mouth only stayed for a moment, separating from hers much too soon.

Then he kissed her again, this time like he meant it. His lips were soft and strong at the same time, molded perfectly to hers. She pressed into him, enjoying this kiss more than she had any other. Fisher gave as much as he took, and she'd never had a man kiss her that way before.

When Stacey entered the wing house at nine-thirty the following morning, Esther already sat in the corner booth. Her brother glanced up from the bar and lifted his towel in a gesture of hello. George nodded toward his sister as if Stacey hadn't already seen her.

She flashed him a smile, because he let them come before

he was open and eat for free. Not that they were ordering copious amounts of hot wings so early in the morning, but Esther did have a box of muffins in front of her and she'd filled two cups with drinks from George's soda machine.

"Hey." Stacey slid into the booth and selected a blueberry muffin covered in large sugar crystals.

"Morning, sunshine." Esther gave her a lopsided smile, and Stacey relaxed. She wasn't sure how Esther would take the news of her new relationship with Fisher, but she couldn't keep it a secret from her best friend. And that smile and that endearment reminded her of exactly that—that Esther *was* her best friend.

Stacey fiddled with the paper on the muffin though she'd only eat the top. She pinched off a piece covered with sugar and popped it into her mouth while Esther scraped her hair into a ponytail. There were unspoken words between them, and Stacey knew Esther would not be the one to break the silence.

"You girls okay here?" George smiled down on them as he set a huge basket of French fries on the table. A platter of dipping sauces came next, and he settled his weight on his back leg.

"Just fine," Esther said, flashing her older brother a smile.

He took the cue and left. Stacey swirled a fry through the spicy ranch sauce and ate it while she worked up her nerve to speak. Esther acted just as dodgy, dunking several fries into the garlic aioli before practically stuffing the whole fistful into her mouth.

That was weird.

"I kissed Fisher DuPont," Stacey blurted, unable to take

the silence and the strange behavior for another moment. "And look, it's not that big of a deal, because it's not like he'll stay interested for long, and I'm sure this is just a summer fling."

Several beats of silence followed her outburst while Esther chewed, swallowed, and stared at her.

"There's no law that says you can't date him," Esther said.

"Well, there kind of is," Stacey said. "At least with you and the other women in the Beach Club."

"It's unspoken, not written."

"So what? I'll have to leave? I won't be invited to meetings anymore?"

Esther shrugged like it was no big deal. "I'm sure some of them will understand."

"Tawny," Stacey said.

Esther consumed another abnormal amount of French fries, this time slathering them with the siracha ketchup. Stacey narrowed her eyes at her. "What's going on with you?"

"Nothing." But her tone of voice screamed *Something! Something huge!*

"Esther," Stacey warned. "You better spill it right now. I told you about Fisher."

Esther sighed and sucked on her straw, draining half the cola in her cup before coming up for air. "All right. There's something."

Stacey put her arms on the table, waiting. Her curiosity drove her toward the brink of madness, but she coached herself to be patient. Breathe deep. Number one, Esther had never held anything back from Stacey. Number two, the way she'd been consuming fried food was so far off the scale of normal that something must be seriously wrong.

"I got asked out on a date."

Surprise lifted Stacey's eyebrows. "Oh. That's not bad. I was expecting you to say you'd been sued or something."

"No, no," Esther said, waving her hand as if swatting at a fly. "Your Ride is fine."

"So. A date." Stacey smiled. "Who was it? How did you let him down gently?" Esther was a master at her excuses so that the men who pursued her didn't feel like she didn't like them. Some of them she was still friends with.

Esther squirmed in her seat. Literally squirmed, something Stacey had never seen her best friend do. Esther was decisive. Take-charge. Letter of the law.

When she remained silent, Stacey said, "Well? Who was it?"

"Marshall Robison." She pushed the basket of French fries away.

"The pineapple plantation Marshall Robison? The man you've driven around the island for two years? The one you have a crush on?" Stacey couldn't believe it. There had to be another Marshall Robison on the island.

Esther nodded, her blue eyes sparking with bright lightning now. "And I didn't let him down gently. I said yes."

Stacey stared, her lungs somehow continuing to breathe on their own. Then she started laughing. Esther joined her, only sobering to say, "You know he and Fisher are good friends, right? We should double."

TWELVE

FISHER ENTERED Owen's office to find it empty. *Strange.* The man seemed to work eighteen-hour days, even with his two teens at home. Fisher had told him countless times to go home at a decent hour, but there always seemed to be some emergency keeping him at the hotel.

Fisher sat in the chair across from Owen's desk to wait. He was a bit early for their Monday morning meeting, and normally Fisher would've tried to skip it. But Stacey had seemed pretty nervous about the storm warning, and Fisher didn't like that he didn't even know about it.

He had the best electronics and WiFi money could buy, and he'd looked up the forecast last night after dropping Stacey back at Aloha Hideaway.

His thoughts scattered as the memory of kissing her stole through his mind. She'd tasted like something salty and something sweet, and he craved the flavor of her mouth right now. They'd agreed he could come to dinner at her bed and breakfast that night, as Mondays were usually slow. She was booked, but she'd already confirmed that morning that only twelve guests had committed to dinner that night.

He could still feel the gentle press of her body against his chest. The careful way she ran her fingernails through his hair—what little he had. He shivered in Owen's office the same way he had in the parking lot at Aloha Hideaway.

"Fisher."

Fisher snapped his eyes open as heat rushed into his face. Owen closed the door behind him, barely glancing at Fisher. "Sorry I'm late."

"Oh, I'm early." Fisher cleared his throat and shifted in his seat. Owen couldn't know what Fisher was thinking, but he still felt like he'd been caught making out with his girlfriend.

Girlfriend.

The word had a nice ring to it. He definitely hadn't had one of those in a while, and he wondered if Stacey would mind the label.

Owen sat behind his desk and slid a folder across it. "New contracts with Your Ride we need to sign. The bagel employees want a raise. Cost analysis is in there. I've got grounds and maintenance working to secure everything possible before the storm tomorrow, and—"

"So we are taking the storm seriously." Fisher tapped the folder as if he could read the documents inside by quick osmosis.

"Of course," Owen said. "You saw the report? It's a tropical storm coming within a few miles of land. The winds are expected to be up to sixty miles per hour—I've assigned you a lower room in which to stay tonight and through Wednesday. The top of the building will sway considerably."

Alarm flowed through Fisher. "I hadn't even thought of that. Have we moved the guests?"

"As low as we can," Owen assured him. "But we're still quite full, and not everyone can be below the tenth floor." He clicked on his computer to wake it. "But the pools will be closed. Anything that can be boarded will be. We've brought in two extra trucks of food and supplies in case people are stuck here after the storm."

He turned his monitor toward Fisher. "The storm surge is what I'm most concerned about. This is a simulation I ran with that nifty piece of software you wrote, and look. With a storm of this size, with winds that high, the storm surge covers the beaches. All of them. All around the bay."

Fisher leaned forward and studied the simulation, which had bright red bleeding up and out of the bay, covering the beaches, the forests along the highway, and extending past the road.

"So it'll come right up to Sweet Breeze?"

"At a depth of three feet," Owen said, his face grave.

"So we can't have people on the first floor either." There were only a handful of rooms on the first floor anyway, what with the lobby, the restaurants, the gym, and other amenities.

"And we'll need to set up a temporary lobby and concierge on the second floor," Fisher added. "Wait. Maybe the fourth. There's more room there with the movie theater and whatnot."

"I think the fourth floor, too, sir." Which meant Owen had already put the wheels to make it so into motion.

"And the employees in the laundry and kitchens?" Those were in the basement. Surely Fisher couldn't ask them to work down there during a tropical storm that would send three feet of storm surge to the base of the hotel.

"Working around the clock to make sure we have what we need. We've reduced our staff for tomorrow by half, to keep everyone safer in their own homes."

Fisher nodded. "I guess I didn't realize how severe this storm was going to be."

"Some people here on the islands don't take the storm warnings seriously." Owen pushed his monitor back into position. "And with the cooler waters that surround the islands, it's possible that the storm will lose some of its steam and not be nearly as bad as the simulation suggests." He gave Fisher a quick look filled with wisdom.

"Better to be safe than sorry," Fisher said.

"My thoughts exactly."

Fisher opened the folder and signed the pages that needed his signature. "I want you and your boys to come here." Owen lived on the edge of the ocean around the curve in the island, and that caused a thick weight of worry to land on Fisher's shoulders.

"Fisher—"

He stilled his pen and looked at his general manager. His friend. "I mean it, Owen. Go get them, pack a bag, whatever. Take a room on the fourth floor."

"The rooms on the fourth floor are full."

Fisher shook his head and scratched the pen across the paper one final time. "Where's my room?"

When Owen didn't answer, Fisher knew it was one of the four executive suites on the fourth floor. "So you and the boys will stay with me."

"I can't—"

"If you're not there by five o'clock when I leave for dinner at Stacey's, I'll hunt you all down." Fisher glared at Owen, who shifted in his seat, looked away, and nodded.

Fisher took the lasered look down a notch. "Good. Because I'm just starting this relationship with this woman and I don't want to cancel with her so I can traipse around this island to find you."

"Yes, sir."

Fisher stood and buttoned his suit coat as he stepped toward the door. "And Owen?"

"Yes?"

"Please don't call me sir." Fisher gave him a warm smile and Owen returned it. "We're friends, and I care about you and the boys."

"I know you do." Owen leaned away from his computer. "So you and Stacey Stapleton?"

"Seems so," Fisher stuffed his hands in his pockets to remain the picture of calmness. His heart started thumping *just* a bit harder than normal though. All at once, it sank to his feet where it rebounded at twice the speed.

"Oh, no." He yanked open the door. "Can you email that simulation to me? I need to warn Stacey."

———

"But you can't stay here." Fisher practically shook his phone at Stacey, pocketing it at the last moment. She would not appreciate that. Not at all.

"Fisher, I've lived here my whole life. This isn't my first tropical storm." She barely glanced at him. Today she wore a shirt the color of lemons, with little white lemon slices all over it. Her shorts were practically microscopic, and the length of her neck that had been exposed called to him. She was really dangerous when she had her hair in a ponytail.

He ground his teeth together. "Stacey."

"Fisher." She looked over the rims of the cute little glasses she wore as she worked on something in a notebook. He didn't look at the writing, didn't want to memorize it.

"Your whole bed and breakfast will be under four feet of water. I have room at my hotel for you, your staff, and all your guests. I'll even give them free breakfast, lunch, and dinner." He bit back the word *please*. He would not beg her, at least not in this situation.

She stood, finally taking him seriously. "Let me see that again."

He handed his phone to her, glad she was actually looking at it this time. The first time, she'd barely even flicked her eyes toward it.

"And the red is the water?"

"It's a prediction," he said. "Things could change, obviously."

She tapped and watched it again, her throat moving as she swallowed. "My entire gardens will flood."

"And it will be raining too," he said. "This is just the storm surge projections."

She handed his phone back to him, her jaw set. Indecision stormed through her beautiful eyes, and Fisher wished there was a way to comfort her. He ached to take her into his arms and whisper to her that he'd take care of everything, take care of her.

The depth of his feelings surprised him, and he forced himself to take a step away from her so he couldn't smell her floral perfume quite so strongly. But this was obviously her office, and the whole room screamed of her, from the hibiscus plants along the back wall, to the frilly curtains on the windows, to the messy desk where she worked. She was beauty in motion, and Fisher found himself slipping a little more down that slippery slope of attraction. Or was that love?

"My parents have to go to work tomorrow."

He shook his head as he thought of her parents going to their job at the volcanic state park—in the mountains. "No. It's supposed to dump up to twelve inches of rain in the mountains."

"That's what they say," she murmured.

He wanted to grab a remote and flip on the TV. Show her that no one was predicting that this storm would settle by much. But she didn't have one in her office. He glanced around, desperate for something he could use to convince her to come to Sweet Breeze so he could make sure she was safe.

She met his eye, and he didn't try to hide his vulnerability. "Stacey," he said. Nothing more.

"I would love some rooms for me and my staff." She lifted her chin. "And my guests. And if I can get my parents to come, them too."

Relief cascaded through him with the force of rushing water, much like he was sure he'd see tomorrow. "Yes, of course. I'll see to it myself."

She lifted her phone to her ear. "I'll call an emergency staff meeting right now. Then I'm calling my parents." She half-turned away from him, and Fisher took that as her silent indication that she wanted him to leave.

He ducked back into the hallway, glancing left and right though he should just turn and go back to the lobby. Stacey lived here, behind one of the two doors at the end of the hall he hadn't seen inside yet.

Though his curiosity burned, he moved in the proper direction, not wanting to violate her privacy—or give her any reason not to trust him, kiss him, and fall madly in love with him.

THIRTEEN

STACEY FELT FRANTIC, like she'd had five minutes to do a job that should've taken five hours. She stared into her overnight bag, wondering what she was forgetting. "It probably doesn't even matter," she muttered. Whatever she needed, Sweet Breeze would have, even in a tropical storm.

Thankfully, her staff had agreed to the accommodations. Most of them would simply stay home with their families, hunker down, and ride out the wind and surf. Stacey, Tayla, and Marge were going to Fisher's hotel to make sure their guests were taken care of. She'd insisted that they share a room on a high floor, but knowing Fisher even the little that she did, she knew she wouldn't be above the fifth floor. She'd probably have her own suite too.

She zipped the bag closed and shouldered it, nothing left to do but meet the guests in the lobby and head down the beach. "All right, guys. Let's go." She looped the leashes of Henry and Hugs around one hand, and scooped up Malificent with the other. The cat hissed, but Stacey simply tucked her more securely under her arm. "No complaining. It's going to rain and you hate getting your paws wet."

She unlooped the leashes and readjusted her bag, then picked up the leashes again. Marge came out of her room just as Stacey did, and the two women exchanged smiles.

"I'm glad we're doing this," Marge said. "The gardens should be okay. We got all the hibiscus harvested, and they know they live in a tropical location."

Stacey was too keyed up to play into Marge's ideas about the plants talking to her. So she simply nodded and gestured for her to go first. She didn't want to leave Aloha Hideaway. It felt like she was abandoning a piece of her soul. Leaving this place was hard, and it was only for a couple of nights, tops. Maybe she could run this bed and breakfast for forty years.

And then what? she wondered. She didn't have anyone to pass it onto the way her grandfather had. Her brother's kids in California barely knew her, and the longing to have a child of her own swept through her so strongly, Stacey sucked in a breath to contain it.

She'd call her parents again once she got to Sweet Breeze. She'd left two messages on both of their phones already, but she hadn't been able to speak to either of them directly. Such a thing wasn't that odd. Her parents worked out in the volcanic fields, and they didn't always have availability to answer calls. But they should be getting home by the time Stacey got settled, and she really needed them to come stay at Sweet Breeze.

Following Marge into the lobby, she found a crowd of

people and their luggage. The scene overwhelmed her, but she drew in a deep breath to center herself. She'd done plenty of hard things in her life, picked herself up when situations tried to kick her down, opened this place with no prior experience in the hospitality industry.

"All right everyone," she said. Her voice barely made a dent in the nervous chatter filling the lobby. She looked at Tayla, who smiled brightly but certainly didn't have a voice that would carry through this mob. Tayla reached out to take Malificent from Stacey, who gladly passed the feline over.

Stacey stepped over to the counter and rang the bell several times. The shrill sound cut through the air, bringing almost everyone to silence. Hugs barked, quieting the last conversations. She glanced around at her guests, a fierce rush of gratitude for their patronage touching her heart.

"All right," she said. "The bus will be here in a few minutes, and we'll get on and get over to Sweet Breeze. They've set up a temporary lobby on the fourth floor, so when you get there, head over to the elevators and go up. I've been assured that they have the best accommodations for us—well, *second* best after Aloha Hideaway." She flashed a smile as several of her guests chuckled and grinned back.

"You have two choices for dinner tonight. There's a restaurant on the first floor that will be open until eight-thirty. It's called…." She glanced at Tayla, who kept her smile in place as she looked steadily back at Stacey.

"I think it's called The Breezeway," Tayla said, her sweet voice lifting into the air. "They serve authentic Hawaiian cuisine, as well as traditional American fare."

"And there's a sushi place on the third floor," Stacey said.

"There will also be a few places you can get drinks and appetizer-type things." Through the front doors, she caught movement. "I think the bus is here. When you get to the hotel, tell them your name, my name, and that you're relocating for two nights from Aloha Hideaway. Okay?"

People nodded and made murmurs of assent.

"Okay." Stacey glanced around at all of them and pulled her schnauzers closer. "Tayla will check you off as you exit. The bus is here."

Tayla grabbed her clipboard, handed the cat to Marge, and took quick strides to the door, where she spoke with each group of guests, marking them off one by one. When only she and Stacey remained in the lobby, Stacey took one last look around. She hoped with everything in her that the next time she walked into Aloha Hideaway, it would look like this.

She'd seen saltwater damage before, and it wasn't pretty. Wasn't cheap to fix either. Didn't happen quickly. She couldn't imagine the catastrophic financial hit she'd take if four feet of water surged through her place.

"Well." She blew out her breath. Nothing she could do about the storm. What would happen, would happen. She'd learned that when she'd discovered that Randy had left her life with a few words in pencil on a piece of paper.

"We have insurance." She met Tayla's eye, and the woman's smile slipped.

"It'll be okay," she said.

"You didn't see the simulation Fisher showed me."

"Did you know he wrote that program?" Tayla returned to the counter and picked up her own bag.

"He did? The one that showed where the flood waters will go?"

"And lots of others," Tayla said. "Software. Apps. That's why he's so rich."

Stacey had not known that. She'd figured that he came from money, had worked for his father in Los Angeles, and had now invested in a beautiful piece of real estate in one of the best vacation locations in the world. All of that could put plenty of zeroes in a person's bank account.

She frowned as she realized she'd just thought of Sweet Breeze as beautiful. She'd disliked it—and the very idea of it —for so long. When had that changed?

Probably about the time you started kissing the owner. The thought reeked of irony, and she shoved it away as she locked the front doors of Aloha Hideaway and turned toward the bus. Henry and Hugs pulled on their leashes, anxious to get out of the weather. But Stacey wanted to see.

A glimmer of the bay could be seen through the fronds to her left. The waves already lapped at the shore with more violence than they normally did, and a shiver crept up Stacey's spine. Relocating was the right thing to do, and once again, a stab of anxiety for her parents hit her lungs.

She climbed onto the bus and the driver brought the doors closed. "Oh." She stalled at the sight of him. "Sterling, right?"

"At your service, ma'am." He smiled and patted Henry's head. "What cute little dogs."

Fisher really did cover all of his bases, and Stacey appreciated him more than ever as she found a seat, settled her pups on her lap, and let his valet drive her and her guests the mile up the road to Sweet Breeze.

She got off first but allowed her guests to enter the hotel ahead of her. By the time she arrived on the fourth floor, only chaos could be seen. There were people everywhere. Some waited in line for food at a few stands that had obviously just been set up. Some waited in line for concessions at the theater. Some waited to get into the movies, as if a storm wasn't only hours away.

And all of her people waited in a roped off line to get checked into their new place. She hoped they didn't like this sterile hotel more than the Hawaiian charm at Aloha Hideaway. What if they did? What if next time they came to the island, they booked here instead of with her?

She couldn't spend her time worrying about things she couldn't control, so she banished the thoughts and waited her turn.

"Stacey Stapleton," she said when she finally made it to the counter. "Marge Mumford and Tayla Lincoln are with me."

The clerk grinned at her, like there was nowhere he'd rather be than standing behind this makeshift counter, checking in someone else's guests. Guests with two small dogs and a very grumpy, still growly cat. Fisher had great employees, that was for sure.

"Welcome to Sweet Breeze," he said before tapping a few times on his keyboard. "Ah, I've got the three of you in your own rooms." He glanced up, not for confirmation, and then clicked. "You're in room five-oh-four. It's got pet accommodations."

He busied himself with getting her room key, the WiFi password, and her meal tickets—one for dinner that night, three for the following day. Stacey just let him do whatever he needed to do, wondering how a room had pet accommodations. After all, it was fruitless to argue with him. The man was doing what the computer told him to, and Fisher had orchestrated that.

He was nowhere to be seen, so Stacey waited until she, Marge, and Tayla all had their room keys, and then they went off in search of their rooms. The fifth floor was much quieter, though there was a museum immediately outside the elevator doors where dozens of people were milling about.

Their rooms were beside each other in the far corner of the hotel, away from the beach. Stacey knew what to expect on the other side of the door, and she got the beautiful carpets, the obscenely high thread count on the sheets, and the honeysuckle soap dispenser in the shower. She also got a litter box under the counter in the bathroom big enough for four cats. She assumed her dogs could go there too, and she wondered how much Fisher paid his employees to clean *that*. More than she could afford, certainly.

After unleashing the dogs, she set her bag on the bed and collapsed beside it. Malificent jumped into the window and hunkered down, clearly not happy with the new arrangements. Henry and Hugs started wrestling near the table, and Stacey laid back on the comfortable bed. Her guests were safe for the night, and she was exhausted.

Before she allowed herself to take a quick cat nap, she dialed her mother one more time.

———

An hour later, Stacey sat cross-legged on the bed, her eyes riveted to the television in room five-oh-four. Marge and Tayla had come over a few minutes ago, and Tayla had told her to turn on the weather.

The storm had arrived, and the outer winds were already reaching the island. Stacey gripped her phone with all the strength she possessed, willing it to chime, ring, buzz, *some*thing.

Her parents were coming, but they weren't here yet.

She'd texted Fisher to say thank you and that she'd arrived, but he hadn't responded. She couldn't imagine how much he was dealing with, so she hadn't started to worry—yet.

Come on, she thought. If her parents didn't arrive soon, they might not be able to get in. The phone in her room had rung fifteen minutes ago, and she'd answered to receive a recorded message in Fisher's voice.

He spoke in a calm, controlled tone and asked all guests to be in the hotel by seven o'clock p.m. "We'll be locking and securing our bottom level at that time," he'd said. "No more guests will be allowed in or out, and we want everyone in Getaway Bay to be safe."

Seven o'clock was only twenty-five minutes from now. Her mother had promised to call the moment they arrived so Stacey could meet them in the lobby and help them get checked in.

She couldn't stay here, gripping her phone and watching the wind strip leaves from the palms along the shore. She tossed the remote control on the bed and stood up. "I'm going down to the lobby. I can't stay here."

Stacey tucked her phone under her bra strap against her collarbone and shoved her feet into a pair of sandals.

"Stacey," Marge said, but Tayla joined her at the door.

"I'll come with you."

"Thank you." Stacey glanced at Marge, who wouldn't be coming. She folded her arms around herself and looked at Stacey with doe eyes. "We'll be back soon."

Down in the lobby, the wide open expanse felt too big, too sterile. Only two Sweet Breeze employees worked at the counter, along with two security guards, who stood at the doors and watched the storm outside.

Stacey approached them as if she would dart outside into the rain. One of the men flung out his arm. "Ma'am, no one goes out."

"Have you seen a couple come in recently? Hawaiian man, white woman, both average height, probably wearing national park clothes?"

He tilted his head to the side. "Yeah, I think so."

Relief rushed through Stacey, but she wouldn't be satisfied until she knew which room her parents were in. "How long ago?" Why hadn't her mother called?

Tayla looped her arm through Stacey's, and Stacey was glad for the friend.

"Ten minutes maybe. They came in with a few other people, and everyone was drenched."

"They went upstairs?"

"Yes."

Stacey exchanged a glance with Tayla, said, "Thank you,"

and turned back to the elevators. Upstairs on the fourth floor, the makeshift lobby harbored much more activity. She looked around for her parents, but she couldn't see them.

Unable to wait another moment or try to find them on her own, she dialed Fisher, hoping he would pick up.

He did with a "Hey, Stacey," in an easy-going voice.

"Can you do me a favor?"

"Of course."

"The security guard downstairs said my parents arrived ten minutes ago, but my mom hasn't called. Can you, I don't know, check your system and see if they checked in and what room they're in?"

Stacey was sure he'd say no, he couldn't look up a guest like that. But he said, "Sure, give me a second."

She heard no clicking, and it seemed like an astronomical amount of time passed before Fisher came back on the line and said, "Room Eleven-seventy-four, Stacey. Checked in seven minutes ago."

True relief flowed through her now, and she exhaled in a long, slow sigh. "Thank you, Fisher."

"So…it might be late, and the building might be swaying, but are we still on for dinner?"

"Dinner." He was supposed to come to Aloha Hideaway for dinner with her and her guests. "Yeah, sure, dinner. But your restaurants are closing at eight-thirty."

"I've already had food sent to my room. It's just across the hotel from you on the fifth floor. But I need, ah, another little while before I'll be ready to give you my full attention."

His full attention sounded fantastic, like a warm blanket she could wrap around her shoulders in this swirling storm.

"I need to go find my parents anyway," she said. "So just text me when you're ready." She hung up and looked at Tayla. "Eleventh floor. You want to come with me to find out why my parents didn't call when they got here?"

Tayla's sunny disposition slipped for the briefest of moments. "Yeah. I like it when you put on your bossy pants."

FOURTEEN

FISHER FELT like he put out a new fire every other second. They still had plenty of rooms in the hotel, but the time to close the doors and secure the property was minutes away. Owen worked beside him, talking into the phone while tapping on his tablet. Fisher wasn't sure what he was dealing with, but as soon as it got solved, another problem would present itself.

Fisher regretted not flagging Stacey's parents, but there was nothing he could do about it now. He'd ordered lasagna —completely unHawaiian, but totally reheatable—an hour ago, and the aroma of it still drifted through the suite where he and Owen worked. The general manager had decided to stay in Marshall's suite, where the boys were currently holed up. Once they finished their work, Fisher would have this room to himself.

Two hours, he told himself. If he could keep the situation from blowing up for two more hours, then he'd get to see Stacey, breathe in the sweet smell of her skin, and relax.

The crowds inside Sweet Breeze didn't seem unruly, at least not from the cameras on his laptop. But there were just *so many* of them, and trying to get them all fed and properly sheltered was no small matter.

Once he and Owen had decided to move everything above the first level, it had taken the full support of the skeleton staff they had at work to move the food, the supplies, the little bars of soap, the extra sheets, blankets, and towels the guests needed.

Fisher was determined to come through this crisis with ten gold stars, so he'd personally hauled four carts of towels from the basement laundry facility up to the second floor himself. The aquarium had been closed, and Fisher had once again, seen to it personally to fill it with the toiletries and other dry goods that didn't need refrigeration.

He rotated his neck, the muscles tight from schlepping boxes, something he hadn't done for a while. But he was actually glad for the opportunity to show his staff that he was willing to do anything he asked them to do.

"It's seven o'clock, sir." The mechanical voice came through the radio sitting on the table between Fisher and Owen.

Fisher picked it up. "Check the perimeter please. Make sure our grounds crew is all accounted for. Then close the doors, Skylar. Lock them down. Put on the sealant." He checked something on the clipboard beside his laptop. "Then I need you on the second floor and Gerald on the fourth."

"Copy that, sir."

The two clerks who'd been assisting stragglers up to the fourth floor came forward and stood at the door. They both held a clipboard and checked people off as they came in, soaking wet despite their rain ponchos. After about ten minutes, Skyler and Gerald returned, also looking worse for the wear, and the radio buzzed again.

"Everyone's inside, sir. Locking the doors now."

Fisher felt very CIA or FBI, like he was running some top secret government facility. He watched the doors slide shut, the power to them get turned off so they wouldn't accidentally trigger, and the manual locks put into place.

Skylar, the bulkier of the two guards, gave the thumbs up to Gerald, and they both turned to pick up a spray can of sealant. It was just a spray caulking that Owen had sent someone to buy at the hardware store, but the Internet said it would work around windows and sliding doors. Whether it was meant to stop surge water from a tropical storm or not, Fisher didn't know, but he would definitely find out.

The weather channel blared from the TV on the wall, the sound muted. He watched as an angry picture of the ocean surrounding the island churned, frothed, and spun on the screen. The captions along the bottom said that the storm had dropped in intensity when it hit the cooler waters surrounding the island, and it was slowly being pushed north and away from the island. But it was currently spinning its wheels right at their front door, and the worst of the storm was expected to hit by ten p.m. that night.

Rain slashed the sky on the screen, and a panning shot showed the strength of the wind as the beautifully woven palm fronds got ripped from the roof of a drink stand on a beach Fisher recognized as being only a couple of miles downshore—closer to where Owen lived than here in Getaway Bay.

The bay did protect them somewhat, but it also made for dangerous surges, so Fisher was glad he'd taken the precautions he had. Relieved Stacey had agreed to relocate all of her guests. Thrilled she'd been able to talk her parents into coming too.

She hadn't seemed too sure of that earlier this morning, when he'd stopped by with his simulation and his worries.

His phone rang, and he pulled himself from the personal thoughts of his girlfriend and her family to focus on his job. If there was one thing Fisher was very good at, it was compartmentalizing. *Work now. Kissing later.*

———

When someone knocked on his door a few hours later, he could barely contain his excitement. His adrenaline had run its course long ago, but it kicked into high gear again as he unlatched the deadbolt and opened the door.

Because Stacey stood in the hallway, her gorgeous red hair spilling over her shoulders. She wore a pair of jeans and a hoodie, and Fisher stared at her. "I didn't know you could actually buy long pants on the island," he said.

"Ha ha." She stepped into his personal space, and a proper gentleman would've backed up to give her room. Fisher had apparently lost his manners, because he didn't move an inch. Her body heat permeated his, and he ran his fingers through her hair.

"Wow, it's good to see you." He leaned down, happy when she tipped up to meet his kiss halfway. He let himself carry on for a moment before realizing they barely stood inside his room, and he was still holding the door open.

He fell back a step or two then. "Come in."

"Busy day." She exhaled and ran her palms down her thighs. "Wow, look at this place."

"Our corner suite." He locked the door after it closed. "You want a tour?"

"Yes, please." She beamed up at him, and Fisher took her hand in his, lifting her fingers all the way to his lips.

"So this is the main living area. Little kitchenette around the corner there." He swept his free hand in that direction as he took her down the short hall and further into the suite. "Full bath as well."

Stacey drank it all in, from the command center evidence still on the couch and coffee table, to the television showing images of the storm.

"Two bedrooms," Fisher said. "They each have their own bathroom, TVs, and temperature controls." He felt foolish staying in this suite when a family could've used it, but Owen had insisted. Fisher's bag sat just inside the door of the bigger bedroom, but Stacey only glanced in before turning back to him.

"It's beautiful." She nodded toward the room service cart. "And what did you order?"

"Oh, right." Fisher sprang into motion, uncovering the lasagna and garlic bread. "I got something I hoped would reheat well. I knew we wouldn't be able to eat until later, and—"

His words stalled when Stacey's fingertips landed on his arm. "What happened?"

He looked down at the angry red marks on his forearm. His hormones raged like the frothing sea on the Weather Channel, and he struggled to remember how he'd gotten injured. "I was helping with boarding up something in the basement. A piece of wood got dropped and scraped along my arm." He pulled it away, though not harshly and somewhat against his will. "I'm fine."

He didn't return to his task of reheating dinner though. Something heated passed between him and Stacey, and while he'd only met her a few days ago, he'd liked everything he'd seen so far. Well, maybe not that fear streak, or the fact that she'd used her past boyfriends as an excuse not to go out with him again. But he understood why she'd done it.

He lowered his head and kissed her again, the magic of the moment almost as powerful as it had been the first time their mouths had touched. His exhaustion, his nerves, the weight he carried, bled out as he deepened the kiss.

He simply couldn't get close enough to her, taste her deeply enough, feel enough of her hair or her skin. "Stacey," he breathed.

She said nothing but pressed into him and kissed him again. If this track continued, he could very well be waking up with her beside him, and the thought both excited and terrified him.

Her fingers worked the buttons on his shirt, and he wrapped his hands around her wrists, stopping the movement. "Stacey," he said again, this time with more power and less air in his voice.

Her eyes drifted open, and Fisher got lost in their depths for a moment. "I don't...I—" Frustration and foolishness combined inside him, a dangerous cocktail that clouded his rational thinking.

"Too soon?" she asked.

"I don't sleep around," he blurted out.

She recoiled like he'd slapped her and wiggled her hands free from his grip. "Oh—wow." She wiped her mouth and paced away from him.

Fisher floundered, trying to figure out what to say to get her to kiss him like that again. But he didn't want that. Did he?

"I just mean," he said carefully, returning to his task of heating up dinner. "That we only met five days ago, and I think we should go a little slower." He gathered up the two plates of lasagna and moved into the kitchenette to put them in the microwave.

"Actually." He turned to face her. "This might seem odd to you, but I've...that is...I...."

"You don't want to have sex with me."

"I do," Fisher said quickly. "But I have, uh, certain assets to protect, and I've made some hasty decisions with the wrong part of my body in the past, and well, I've determined not to repeat those mistakes." He hoped that didn't make him a giant jerk. Or pathetic.

Stacey stared at him, her mouth falling open slightly. "Assets?"

"It's why I don't drink anymore either." He turned when the microwave beeped and took out the first plate, replacing it with the second. He collected the green salads and the sodas from the fridge and took them to the table.

He hated this part of his past. "So before Juliana, I was dating this woman named Gigi. At least I thought we were dating. We went out to all these clubs and bars all the time, slept over at each other's houses, even said I love you." He shrugged. "She was just waiting for the perfect time when I was a little too drunk and a little too out of it before she got me to sign some bogus document to half of my estate."

He kept his back to her as he fiddled with the silverware, glad when the microwave beeped again and he had a concrete task to focus on. "Of course, I have enough money to pay for good lawyers, and nothing really damaging came out of it. I lost myself for a while." His voice trailed off, and he remembered that who he'd become after Gigi was a win.

"But I pulled myself back together. Got back to developing apps, and put my *brains* to good use."

"I'm so sorry." Stacey's voice sounded tiny, like she'd whispered into the great big universe.

"But now I don't drink, and I don't fool around with women, and my life is all very straight-laced." He set the second plate of lasagna on the table and plucked up the courage to face her.

She lifted her chin, that defiant glint in her eye that turned Fisher all the way to high. "So are you and I just fooling around?"

"*I* don't think so," he said. "What do you think?"

She pressed her lips together and shook her head.

"I do think we need more than five days together before we go down that road," Fisher said, hopefully with as much kindness in his voice as he could muster. "But don't think I don't want to, or that I don't trust you."

He didn't know how to articulate himself, so he simply sat down and said, "Wow, I'm hungrier than I thought."

Stacey joined him, and he cast her a quick smile. "Sorry," she said again.

He covered her hand with his. "You don't have anything to be sorry about."

She looked at him, a perfect storm of emotions swirling in the depths of her green eyes. "I trust you too," she finally said, and a smile burst onto Fisher's face.

He leaned over and gave her a sweet kiss, something slow and meaningful and what he hoped would convey how he wanted to be with her. Nothing frantic. Nothing too rushed. He wanted to spend time with her, get to know her, fall in love with her before he made love with her.

By the time he pulled back, he was pretty sure she'd gotten that message. Her face held a pretty blush, and their lasagna was lukewarm again. He dug in anyway, his own heart pattering around in his chest in a strange way. A way that told him he had already started the fall.

FIFTEEN

STACEY LAY in the circle of Fisher's arms, listening to him breathe in…and exhale. He'd fallen asleep ten minutes into the movie he'd ordered, exactly as he'd said he would. Stacey didn't mind. There was something oddly comforting about having him asleep beside her. The scent of his skin filled her nose, and she smiled in the darkness.

She should go. Get up and tiptoe toward the door without waking him. But she also knew he needed his rest and he wouldn't get it on the couch in the living room when the bed in the suite was so much better.

Assets to protect.

His words rang through her mind no matter how she tried to push them out.

I trust you.

She'd felt the truth in both statements, and she admired the fact that he'd made mistakes in the past but wasn't willing to repeat them. He'd been affectionate toward her, and the smoldering, slow kiss he'd given her before they'd started to eat got her internal temperature skyrocketing again. If he made love the way he kissed, she could definitely wait.

The windowpane shook with another blast of wind, and Stacey looked at her phone. Ten-forty-five. The worst of the storm was upon them, and Fisher was sleeping through it. Having such a competent staff and flawless preparations could clearly do that for a man.

Stacey closed her eyes and tried to sleep too. But her own actions from earlier that night haunted her. Why had she thrown herself at him like that? She knew she wasn't ready to sleep with him, and yet—she shook her head.

The real reason sat just behind her tongue and she didn't want to admit it. Not to herself. Not to him. Not to anyone.

If she slept with him, their relationship could be over. And Stacey was terrified of falling in love with him—something that had already started to happen.

And falling in love was weak. Falling in love meant she was willing to get her heart broken. Falling in love meant she'd come home one day and find him gone, or see him kissing another woman, or even if it did work out, he'd leave her in a decade for someone better.

If Stacey hadn't experienced all of those things herself, she had close friends who had.

Slowly, carefully, so she wouldn't wake Fisher, she typed a text to Esther. *Safe tonight?*

Yes. You.

Physically.

What happened?

Stacey stared past the brightly lit screen, her eyes absorbing only blackness. She could sum up how she felt in one word. *Scared.*

Of?

Stacey had always been able to be frank with Esther, and she needed that now more than ever. *Falling for him.*

Several minutes passed before Esther's response came in. It was so short, it shouldn't have taken her so long to type. *Maybe it's time we let go of the past.*

Stacey cradled her phone against her chest, the light dimming so only the TV flashed in the room.

"Maybe," she whispered to herself. This time, when she closed her eyes, she was able to fall asleep.

———

When she woke, her neck complained loudly of its cramped position. She moaned, slowly coming to consciousness, and startled, trying to figure out where she was.

Her back was hot—like, really hot, and there was something heavy on her hip.

"Fisher," she said. The TV had turned blue at some point, casting an eerie glow on the two of them. She sat up, disturbing Fisher as she did.

He groaned too, and she said, "Fisher," again to get him to wake up. His eyes fluttered open, and when he saw her, the softest look of love painted across his face. "Hey, sweetheart. What time is it?"

Stacey didn't know, because she couldn't find her phone.

She wiped her hair off her face and tucked it behind her ears. "Not sure. Late."

He reached for her, and she let him pull her to him for one of those sultry kisses that left her weak everywhere. "I'll walk you back to your room."

"I don't know where my phone is," she said against his lips, glad when he formed his mouth to hers once again.

"Mm." He kissed her like he was one breath away from dying and she was his only source of oxygen. He finally broke their connection and said, "I'll help you find it." He reached behind his head and snapped on the lamp, flooding the room with light.

Stacey flinched away from it and spotted her phone on the floor. She scooped it up, suddenly anxious to get back to her own room. "It's barely midnight," she said, a bit relieved. That wasn't a walk-of-shame time to go home from a date that hadn't even started until nine-thirty.

He switched off the TV and put his shoes back on. He was wonderfully handsome fresh from sleep, his features soft and his movements a little slow. She liked this vulnerable side of him—liked nearly everything about him.

They took the stairs to the fifth floor and he leaned into the wall outside her door. "Good night, Stacey." He spoke her name with a hint of deep emotion in his voice, and Stacey wrapped her arms around him.

"Thank you," she whispered. It was an expression of gratitude for everything he'd done for her. For accommodating her guests. For dinner. For holding her on the couch. For refusing to sleep with her. For giving her a third chance at discovering if she could fall in love and survive.

———

The storm blew itself out by dawn, and Stacey stood at the window in her room, all of her animals lined up on the windowsill. Hugs stood on his hind legs, his front paws on the glass as if eager to go out and explore.

Stacey wasn't, and she couldn't see the bay or her bed and breakfast from her position. Nerves pricked every organ in her body, and she should go downstairs and get back down the beach to her own place. Then she could see what the storm had done and stop worrying about what it *might* have done.

But she didn't want to go alone. She turned at the same time someone knocked on her door. Part of her wanted it to be Fisher, but she knew he'd be too busy to walk through Aloha Hideaway with her.

She opened the door to find her parents standing in the hall. "Morning, sweetheart." Her mom hugged her and her dad handed her a poppyseed bagel sandwich with bacon and eggs.

"Hey Mama." Stacey took comfort in the familiar scent of her mother's clothes. Part powdery and part volcanic rock, Stacey loved the smell of her mom.

"We thought you'd like some company to go through your grandfather's house." Her dad lifted his to-go cup of coffee to his lips.

"I would, thanks. Let me get Tayla and Marge, and we'll all head over there." Her guests had another night at Sweet Breeze if they needed it, but the storm hadn't been as bad as the weather reports had predicted. Maybe they could all get back to Aloha Hideaway tonight, with Betty cooking up her famous pork buns and sticky rice.

She slipped her feet into sandals, texted her co-workers, and leashed the schnauzers. Ten minutes later, she met Marge and Tayla in the lobby on the first floor, where the doors leading outside were wide open. There was no evidence of water damage of any kind, and either Fisher's sealing methods had worked, or the storm surge hadn't come this high.

Hope worked through her, but she tamped it down. She would assume the worst until she saw the sprawling estate for herself. She had more than just the building to worry about, and the rain last night had been torrential.

It only took a few minutes to get around the curve in the bay before her father turned down the lane that led to the small parking lot outside of Aloha Hideaway. The sun shone brightly on the wet ground, making it shine like oil.

"This side looks okay." She had a feeling she'd be doing a lot of talking to herself today, as no one answered her. Marge headed around the west side of the property, toward the gardens, and Stacey let her go.

Tayla approached the front doors, which also looked like they hadn't held back any saltwater, and unlocked them. Stacey joined her in the doorway, her eyes scanning, darting, volleying, back and forth, searching for any damage. She took a deep breath, hoping she wouldn't smell wet carpet or wood.

"It looks okay," Tayla said, her voice almost as bright and bubbly as normal.

Stacey stepped inside the lobby, which seemed exactly

the same as it had been when she'd left yesterday. "I'll take the guest wing," she said. "And my suite. Will you check the kitchens and the rest of the east wing?"

"Sure thing."

Stacey ran her fingertips along the check-in counter as she headed over to the guest entrance. Everything seemed okay, and she allowed the dormant hope to grow roots and take seed in her heart.

All five guest rooms and bathrooms were untouched by the storm, and Stacey spoke aloud as she checked off each of them and their amenities. Her suite was likewise undamaged, and when she met her parents in the lobby, she said, "What does it look like outside?"

"Come see." Her father turned and went through the front door, the grim look on his face erasing the buoyancy Stacey had infused into her step.

The gardens had definitely not fared as well as the house. The palms along the gate all had broken branches, with fronds and leaves littering the ground. The bushes and flowers looked like they'd had an avalanche of gravel dumped on them, but there were no rocks left behind.

Puddles marred the flower beds, as well as several low lying places in the lawn. Stacey saw Marge up ahead, walking slowly down the rows of hibiscus. "How's it looking, Marge?"

The woman turned, her expression grave. "They'll recover, but we'll lose a few weeks of crops."

Stacey folded her arms, the temperature in the shady garden chillier now that she'd seen the damage. "We'll all get out here today to help get this place cleaned up."

Marge took a few steps closer, her sky blue eyes earnest. "I'd like to direct the cleanup, if that's all right."

"Of course," Stacey said. "I'll get you the people, you tell us what to do."

Marge nodded, bent down and cradled a broken leaf on one hibiscus plant, leaning closer as if to hear something. Stacey turned away, hopeful that she could at least keep her bookings for the next few months. She had a wedding on the calendar in only three weeks, but she felt confident the gardens could be restored by then.

"Okay." She blew out her breath. "Let's go let our guests know they can come back to Aloha Hideaway."

SIXTEEN

FISHER STOOD out of the way in the lobby, watching his employees and guests get back to normal. The concierge and check-in attendants were all back in position. Guests who were supposed to check out today were leaving, as were the two hundred extra people they'd taken in for the night.

The steady stream of people felt overwhelming, but it also energized Fisher in a way he hadn't expected. He'd put this place together singlehandedly, without the help of his father, and he was pretty proud of that.

Fisher pushed the pride away, knowing it usually put him in a place he didn't want to be. He'd always thought he had a big enough head just because of his genetics, and he didn't need anything adding to that.

He'd slept little after taking Stacey back to her room, but he couldn't pinpoint the reason why. Her parents had checked out early, but as far as he knew, Stacey was still on the guest list. He'd asked his lead team member on the check-out desk to text him as soon as she did, because he was hoping to ask her how Aloha Hideaway had fared the storm.

Sweet Breeze had some cleanup to do on the grounds, where Fisher had already deployed his grounds crew. They'd probably have it done by the time the sun reached its pinnacle, and he toyed with the idea of offering their time to Stacey. Because if his grounds had suffered, hers were probably in complete disarray. She had dozens more trees, all those flowers, and the tropical forest that could produce a ton of debris when there was simply a stiff wind.

His phone went off, and he glanced at it. *Stacey Stapleton just checked out.*

Fisher scanned the streams of people coming and going, but he didn't see Stacey's beautiful red hair. His phone buzzed again, and he almost ignored it. He was glad when he glanced down and saw the message.

She'd like to speak with you. I put her in Owen's office for now. Should I have her wait?

I'm on my way now. Fisher stepped away from the pillar where he stood, wondering why Stacey needed to see him. Why she couldn't text him herself. Why she needed to be isolated in an office.

His steps became less sure the closer to Owen's office he got, and he didn't make it past the counter before Tom, his check-out lead, intercepted him. "Miss Stapleton seemed... upset," he said. "That's why I put her in Owen's office."

Fisher tried to hear more in the man's words. "Upset about what?"

"I'm not sure, sir. But Vicki didn't know what to do and flagged me down."

Fisher nodded. "Thank you, Tom. Apologize to Vicki for me." He continued down the hall and behind the counter, where Owen's closed office door met him. He wasn't sure what was going on, but he'd entered conference rooms with hostile business owners, angry clients, and more.

He could handle Stacey Stapleton.

I hope.

He knocked a couple of times and twisted the knob. "Stacey?" The door opened slowly to reveal Stacey standing at the fish tank, her back to him. "Can I come in?"

"It's your hotel." Her tone carried enough ice to freeze all the water in the bay.

He entered and closed the door behind him. No wonder Tom had isolated her. They didn't need her causing a scene in the very crowded lobby.

"What's going on?" he asked.

She spun from the tropical fish, her brilliant eyes flashing with fury. "Two of my guests don't want to come back to Aloha Hideaway."

Fisher blinked, unsure of how to respond. Or how this was his fault. He pocketed his hands and rocked back on his heels. "I'll compensate you for the rooms."

"It's not about the money." She took a step toward him, and Fisher knew there was nothing he could say or do to make this better. She was angry, and determined to be.

"I'm sorry, Stacey."

"You're sorry?" She laughed, but it wasn't charming or

playful or wonderful, the way he'd heard before. "They would've been fine at my place."

"I was trying to help everyone be safe during the storm."

"Yeah, with your fancy simulations." She shook her head and scoffed. "I can't believe I—" She pressed her lips together and looked away. When her eyes came back to his, they held a hint of resignation. "You know what? I will take your money." She started toward him, and he stepped out of the way so she could open the door.

She pulled it open, paused, and looked up at him, her beautiful eyes filled with pain.

"Don't go," he said. Just last night, she'd almost ripped his buttons as she tried to undress him. How was this his fault?

"I'm...I have work to do on my property."

"I'd like to come help."

"I can handle it."

"I have no doubt about that." Fisher wanted to reach up and tuck the errant lock of hair that had fallen out of her messy bun. He fisted his fingers instead. "But I'd still like to help. I've already spoken to my head groundskeeper, and he can have a crew of six men over to Aloha Hideaway this afternoon."

Emotions stormed across Stacey's face. She opened her mouth to protest, no doubt, but Fisher said, "I'll send them anyway."

She didn't need to know that he hadn't yet spoken to Patrick about sending the crew over. He studied her, buoyed by the fact that she hadn't left yet.

"How did your place fare?" he asked.

"The house itself is intact. No water damage." She folded her arms, the fight leaving her. "It's just my gardens that need work."

Fisher nodded. "I'll send my guys over."

"Marge gets to be in charge."

"Of course." He tilted his head, trying to figure her out. She seemed like a puzzle he couldn't solve in this moment, and he could fix a Rubix cube without even touching it. "Can I take you to lunch later?"

"I have no idea when I'll be able to go."

At least it wasn't a no.

"I'm at the mercy of your schedule." He hated the formality between them. Hated that he hadn't touched her. Hated that she'd lost customers because of him and Sweet Breeze. "I don't want to start over."

"What?"

"Why are you mad at me?"

Stacey sighed and ducked her head. "I'm sorry. I'm not mad...at you."

"I'm glad to hear it." He reached out and brushed her fingers with his. A whisper of a touch that lasted only a moment.

She moved back into the office and closed the door. "I'm sorry."

"No need to apologize." Fisher opened his arms, relieved when Stacey stepped into them and laid her head against his chest.

"I just got frustrated. When you started building this place, I thought I might lose customers to Sweet Breeze. But I still stayed booked, so I stopped worrying about it."

"You stayed here last week," he reminded her.

"Yeah, I stayed here last Thursday. I just wanted to see for myself. It's a beautiful hotel, and yes. I thought I might lose some customers to you, but then the room service guy barged into my room, and I stopped worrying again."

He chuckled and tightened his grip around her. "There's plenty of business for both of us. I don't do weddings."

"Like, personally you're not looking to get married? Or Sweet Breeze doesn't help people tie the knot?"

Fisher's pulse skipped a beat. "Sweet Breeze doesn't accommodate the actual nuptials."

Stacey stepped back but kept her hands solidly on his shoulders. "And you?"

"I'm not fundamentally against the idea of marriage." Fisher could be political when he had to be. He'd only started dating Stacey. The I do's were very far away on the horizon, if she could stop blaming him and his hotel.

"I want a burger for lunch," she said.

"I'm sure we can make that happen."

"So I'll text you?"

"Absolutely."

Stacey stretched up and skated her lips across his cheek. Then she slipped out the door, leaving him in the office alone. He turned away from the wood and approached the fish tank where Stacey had been standing.

He liked her. A lot. Probably more than he should at only six days into the relationship. He liked that she wasn't perfect. That she liked him enough to unbutton his shirt. That she got upset when she lost customers to him. That she cared so much about her property that she was willing to accept his help.

"What would happen if we got married?" he asked the fish. It was a question he needed to ask her. He couldn't see her giving up her grandfather's house and coming to stay on the twenty-eighth floor with him. Could he see himself moving into her house?

The door opened behind him, and he turned to find Owen entering with Marshall. "Oh, he is in here." They both looked at him with surprise, and Fisher simply put his hands in his pockets.

"We made it through the storm." He had a feeling another one was coming, but not from Mother Nature.

"Sure did." Owen settled behind his desk and proceeded to ignore the other two men.

"Can I talk to you?" Marshall asked. "Have you been back up to your suite yet?"

"Not yet. Let's go get my bag and head up there."

"Can you get some of those spinach soufflés sent up?"

"Owen?" Fisher asked.

The general manager picked up the phone and pushed a button. Fisher heard him say, "Four spinach soufflés for Mister DuPont," as he followed Marshall out of the office.

———

Fisher's hands rotated the panels on a Rubix cube he'd picked up as soon as he'd entered his suite. He didn't normally discuss his relationships with anyone, but he'd never had one as complicated as the hot-then-cold thing he had going with Stacey. And Marshall didn't date either—at least no one more than once—so Fisher wasn't sure if he was the best man to talk to anyway.

He sighed and slumped onto Fisher's couch. "You signed new contracts with Your Ride?"

"Sounds familiar." With everything going on with the storm, Fisher wasn't sure what he'd signed the other day.

"Do you know the owner?"

"Esther Pinnett, sure. Does a lot of the driving herself."

"She does all of my driving," Marshall said. "And she's Stacey's best friend."

Fisher looked away from the colored squares on the cube. "I didn't know that."

"I'm going out with her on Thursday."

Fisher abandoned the Rubix cube completely. "Esther? You?"

"Don't sound so shocked."

"What party do you have coming up?"

"This isn't for a party." Marshall drummed his fingers on the table and wouldn't meet Fisher's eye.

"I've never seen you pay any attention to women for anything but business."

"I could've said the same for you." Marshall looked at him out of the corner of his eye. "But now you've got Stacey staying with you until all hours of the night."

Fisher scoffed. "I do not." And how would Marshall know anyway? Maybe Stacey had said something to Esther already, and she'd told Marshall? Was that what he wanted? A gossipy girlfriend who told her best friend everything about them?

"That's not what Owen said."

"Owen doesn't need to monitor me twenty-four-seven."

Marshall chuckled. "Well, he does."

Fisher knew he did, and it had never bothered him. Until now. "It was barely past midnight," he said. "And I was asleep for at least two hours before that."

"Sounds romantic."

Fisher could still feel the ghost of Stacy's fingers against his chest, and the awkward conversation that had followed. No, last night hadn't been terribly romantic, except for those couple of kisses where she let him explore her mouth completely.

"You like her?" Marshall asked.

"I do."

Marshall nodded. "We're not normal men, you know? There's so much to consider when getting involved with a woman." He exhaled like he'd been up all night, same as Fisher.

He returned his attention to his Rubix cube, wishing he could solve his situation with Stacey as easily as he could make the sides line up.

His phone went off, and he read the text from Stacey before tipping it toward Marshall.

"Lunch at noon?" Marshall read. "Tell her I'm busy." He leaned back into Fisher's couch and closed his eyes.

Fisher scoffed and started typing on his phone. "Yeah, I can see that. Real busy." He stared at the neat blue stickers he'd been able to arrange perfectly, wishing he could do the same with all aspects of his life.

"Are you taking Esther to the family dinner?" he asked. "Or skipping it?"

"Skipping it."

He joined his friend as he relaxed and closed his eyes, his text sent. Maybe nothing had changed between him and Stacey. She'd just been frustrated about the situation and directed it at him. It certainly wasn't the first time Fisher had been the target of misdirected anger.

But since their talk last night, and their siesta on the couch together, something felt like it had shifted inside him. Inside their relationship. And he didn't know what it was, or how to get it to line up again.

SEVENTEEN

STACEY WATCHED Marge as she picked up one leaf at a time. At this rate, it would take six months just to get the branches and fronds cleared from the gardens. As soon as she'd calmed down about the loss of her two guests, she'd put the rooms back up for vacancy, and they'd both been booked within an hour.

Foolishness raced through her at her behavior toward Fisher. It certainly wasn't his fault that her guests had decided to stay at his hotel. But she'd been stunned and angry when she found out, and he was the only one around to take the brunt of her frustration.

She'd apologized; he hadn't seemed like it would be a problem, but Stacey still felt stupid. He'd just confirmed their lunch date, and he'd asked her to it, so he couldn't be too mad. A man like Fisher probably had dozens of people upset with him at any one time, a fact she knew because of how he'd handled her outburst.

Sorry about earlier, she typed out. Would she be too needy if she sent it? She really had been out of the dating scene for too long, and she had no idea what she was doing.

Maybe stop doing it then. The thought floated through her mind, and she wondered what she meant. Stop apologizing? Or stop dating Fisher altogether?

"Hey, there you are."

Stacey turned at Esther's familiar voice. She sidled up to Stacey and put her arm around her shoulders. "How was last night?"

Stacey drew in a big breath and blew it out. "Okay."

"That doesn't exactly sound like a woman who's madly in love with her new boyfriend."

"I'm not good at relationships." Stacey stepped toward the beach, moving sideways around a puddle. Esther went with her, and when the warm sand seeped between her toes, Stacey felt the familiarity melt into her bones. This was what she could do. Sit on the beach. Chat with her friends. Sip fruity drinks from Two Coconuts. Watch the waves roll in.

"I'm way out of my league with him." She didn't let her gaze drift down the beach to Sweet Breeze. Because of the curve in the bay, she wouldn't be able to see anything but the top few floors.

Esther scoffed and linked her arm through Stacey's. "Don't say that. You're a great catch. He's lucky to even know your name." They stood on the beach, the waves gently lapping the shore. When Stacey turned around to go back through the gate, she saw the line of water on the fence posts. It was about eight inches up and indicated there had been some storm surge.

She heard yapping back toward the house, and she turned that way. "Thanks, Esther."

"Are you going to break up with him?"

"I don't know." She almost had that morning, then he'd said two words that had stopped her.

Don't go.

Neither Randy nor Malik had ever asked her to stay in their lives. And here Fisher was, saying it within a week of their relationship. But if she didn't go, she felt certain he would, eventually.

And yet she still wanted to have lunch with him. She felt twenty pieces short of a jigsaw puzzle that needed every bit to be just right for the picture to make sense. Gazing out over the bay she loved, Stacey wished her grandmother and grandfather were still here, right here on this patch of beach, with her.

She'd spent so many carefree days with them, building sandcastles as a child, then sunbathing as a teenager, and then working in the hibiscus gardens with her grandfather. She'd slept in every room in the sprawling house, and when she learned he'd left it to her, Stacey had experienced true happiness in a world where her heart had been broken.

"I didn't think I needed anything else," she said to the breeze, the waves, her best friend. "And I love you. You know I love you." Stacey turned from the waves and looked into Esther's piercing blue eyes. "Is it bad if I say I'm lonely, and Fisher helps me feel a little...less lonely?"

"Oh, honey. Of course not." Esther hugged her arm and leaned her head against Stacey's shoulder. "I spend so much of my time wearing power suits and being professional, I'm not even sure I know how to let my hair down."

"I'm sure Marshall can help you with that." Stacey hipped her friend, feeling lighter now that she'd admitted she was lonely, and that Fisher eased some of that.

"We'll see."

"When are you going out with him?"

"Thursday." Esther pulled in a breath that made a hissing sound. "I hope I know what I'm doing."

"Of course you do. Your two years of sitting silently in the front seat are finally over, Esther." She twisted and grinned at her friend. "Now, tell me that I should enjoy my summer with Fisher."

They started walking back to the bed and breakfast, with Esther saying, "You should enjoy this summer with Fisher."

———

Stacey did enjoy her time with Fisher. They ate meals together, walked on the beach together, held hands whenever they went out. With the help from his grounds crew, the gardens at Aloha Hideaway were cleaned up and flourishing within a few days.

The weddings she had on her schedule for the end of June went swimmingly, and everything at Aloha Hideaway hummed along as normal. The only thing that wasn't normal was Fisher's continual adoration of her.

He sent flowers on days he couldn't see her in person. On days they did get together, he greeted her with wide smiles and soft kisses, leaving her feeling cherished and wanted,

ALOHA HIDEAWAY INN   183

two things she hadn't felt in years. Not even when she was with Malik and Randy. No one had ever treated her the way Fisher did, like she was royalty and deserved the very best.

As June moved into July, Stacey was starting to think her summer fling could become serious by autumn. Every time she thought about it, she freaked out. So she'd stopped thinking about it on the Fourth of July, with red, white, and blue fireworks popping above her head as she kissed Fisher on the beach.

She sighed and tucked herself against his chest. She'd had a couple of meetings with her Beach Club, and no one had said anything about her relationship with Fisher. Esther's dates with Marshall had stayed on the down-low too. But the club had to know. Stacey hadn't kept their dates out of the public eye, and Fisher drew everyone's gaze wherever they went.

"Stacey, we're almost out of the white chocolate popcorn."

Stacey turned toward Tayla's voice, catching the rows and rows of chairs they'd set up on their private beach, and the tables in the back held a variety of popcorns, sodas, and other treats for the festivities.

"Is there more in the kitchen?"

"Betty can't find her key."

Confused, Stacey eased away from Fisher, glad when he kept his fingers on hers for as long as possible, and headed back to the tables. She had personally stood with Betty in the kitchen that afternoon, coating popcorn with white chocolate and drizzling it with red and white streaks. She'd eaten her fair share of the treat, and she wanted more right now. Oh, how she loved chocolate-covered popcorn, and the bowl here was empty, so her guests obviously enjoyed it too.

"Let me go check." She headed back through the gate and down the path toward the house, wondering why Betty needed a key at all. Aloha Hideaway shouldn't be locked, as guests could come and go as they pleased, even during the festivities hosted by the bed and breakfast.

But she found Betty pacing near the front doors, wringing her hands. "Oh, Stacey," she said as Stacey approached. "It's locked, and I can't get in."

Stacey didn't have keys either, and she tried the doorknob though she didn't doubt Betty. "Okay." She turned around, searching her mind for a solution. "I don't really know how it could've gotten locked."

"Me either."

Stacey couldn't even remember who had been last out. Tayla, Betty, and two other employees had helped set up the party, and Fisher had even carried out the huge metal tub of soda cans, bottled lemonades, and tropical fruit juices. He hadn't been last out though.

"I'll call a locksmith," she said, pulling out her phone. "It's fine, Betty. Don't worry."

The older woman still looked near panic, so Stacey said, "Why don't you go on back to the party? There are other treats and plenty of drinks. Would you ask Fisher to come talk to me?"

Betty nodded and bustled away, but Fisher didn't come back. Minutes passed, and Stacey hung up with Lester the Locksmith, satisfied that he was on his way. But why wasn't Fisher? She'd hoped he'd be able to somehow work his billionaire magic and get the door unlocked without her having to pay someone.

A cry of delight went up from the crowd as the dark sky filled with a spectacular display of fireworks. She moved back toward the beach, but she couldn't find Fisher. He normally stood tall enough for her to pick out in a crowd. Maybe he was sitting.

No one seemed put out about the lack of chocolate covered popcorn, and Stacey turned back to Aloha Hideaway, hoping Lester would show up so she could get her place open before the guests started to come back. After all, it was creeping closer to eleven with every passing minute, and the Independence Day festivities would end soon.

Stacey pulled out her phone to send Fisher a message, but Lester's van pulled up, his headlights nearly blinding her. She shoved her phone in her back pocket and went to meet the locksmith.

"I don't know what happened," she said. "But my front door is locked, and I need it unlocked."

"Do you own this place?" Lester scanned her from head to toe and looked at the intricately carved sign with the hibiscus flowers stained purple.

"Yes," she said. "I'm Stacey Stapleton, and I just need the front door unlocked before my guests come back from the beach."

"I'm going to need to see some ID."

Frustration washed through her. "I live here too—only half of the house is for guests—and I left my purse inside."

"So you don't have ID." He settled his weight on his left foot like there was no hurry to anything.

Stacey cocked her hip, mirroring the locksmith, the glow from the lights illuminating his disbelieving face and dark hair. "If you unlock the front door, I'll grab my purse and show you any ID you want. *And* pay you."

"Anyone who can vouch for you?"

If Fisher were here, he could. And Stacey was willing to bet her next hibiscus crop that Lester wouldn't be questioning her if Fisher stood at her side in the first place. She crossed her arms and glared. "Sure. Let me text my staff down at the beach."

She made a group text for Betty, Tayla, and Marge to come help her get the bed and breakfast unlocked. A few minutes later, all three of them arrived wearing varying degrees of concern on their faces.

"This is Betty, my head chef," Stacey said. "Tayla, who runs the front desk. And Marge, my lead horticulturist." She gestured to Lester. "Can you guys tell him who I am?"

"Stacey Stapleton?" Tayla guessed.

"She owns this place," Betty said, her voice tight.

Lester lifted one shoulder like he didn't care either way and approached the door. Stacey watched him with a bit of triumph and a lot of frustration.

She tore her attention from Lester as he got to work on the lock. "Hey, Tayla, where's Fisher?"

"I thought he was here," she said.

"Betty." Stacey turned toward her chef, her concern for her boyfriend lifting like helium filled balloons. "Did you ask him to come back here?"

"When I got back to the beach, he was gone." Betty

looked apologetic. "I'm sorry, Stacey. I thought we must've crossed paths in the gardens."

Stacey's concern morphed into worry, and she practically punched her phone in her haste to dial Fisher. The line rang, and rang, and rang. He didn't pick up, and Stacey was forced to hang up before she could leave a message when Lester gave a yelp and the front door of Aloha Hideaway swung in.

He wore a look of extreme pride as she approached. "How much for your services?"

"One-fifty."

"Thank you. Let me go get my purse for that ID."

"That's not—"

Stacey silenced him with a glare and stepped past him. She dialed Fisher again as she hurried down the hall toward her suite, but again, he didn't answer. "Fisher," she said. "It's Stacey. Where did you go? One minute you're at the beach, and the next you're gone. Please call me."

She pushed into her suite, very aware that her heart was pounding entirely too fast. She couldn't help the wall of emotions that hit her like a tsunami. She blinked and she could see the single sheet of paper taped to the front door.

Blink.

I'm sorry, Stacey.

Blink.

I can't stay here.

Blink.

Her heart seemed to physically crack, making a horrible breaking sound, as she read the note from Randy. She remembered sitting at the table for hours, holding the note by the edges as if keeping it pristine would mean it wasn't true.

She'd never seen him again. She had no idea if he lived on another island in Hawaii, or was backpacking through Peru, or living on the mainland. For a long time, she used to wake up every morning and wonder where he was. It took a long time to stop loving Randy, and Stacey wasn't willing to lose more years of her life like that.

"Fisher hasn't left the island," she told herself as she strode across the room and plucked her purse from the dresser. She'd pay Lester, make sure her guests were comfortable for the night, and then she'd find Fisher.

EIGHTEEN

FISHER DIDN'T STOP by Sweet Breeze to pack a bag. He had credit cards in his wallet and his phone. He could buy anything he needed on his way home to Michigan.

It's your mom....

The words reverberated through his mind, echoing and endless, haunting and hollow. He wasn't going to answer the call from his father, but he was now extremely glad that he had. Why Denver hadn't called, Fisher wasn't sure. Probably because he was in the hospital with Fisher's mother, and another wave of worry rolled over him. His father hadn't known much, but he'd gotten enough pieces to put together that Fisher's mother had been in a car accident and her injuries were serious.

Fisher grabbed his belt, wallet, and phone from the bucket he'd put them in to go through the machine at the airport. Stuffing everything in his pockets and looping his belt around his waist, he grabbed his shoes. It felt like everything took too long. The simple act of putting on his shoes felt like it would delay him from getting to his mom.

He was irrational, and he knew it, but his blood bubbled through his body like it would cause him to explode at any moment. The only flight out of Hawaii tonight was to Portland, but Fisher didn't care. He'd fly wherever the plane was going. He just had to get off this island.

Thirty minutes later, he was in his seat, his phone in airplane mode, and his anxiety higher than it had ever been.

He wanted to talk to Stacey, just to hear her voice one more time before flying over the Pacific Ocean to the mainland. Owen would get the message to her, and Fisher would call her as soon as he landed.

That will have to do, he thought as he leaned his head back and ignored the preflight lectures about water landings.

A thunderstorm—"rare, but not completely unusual," according to the pilot—kept the plane in the air for an extra forty-five minutes, and by the time they landed, Fisher's phone updated to six-thirteen a.m. It would be three-thirteen in Hawaii, and he couldn't disturb Stacey in the middle of the night.

Owen will tell her. Owen will tell her. Owen will tell her.

He stepped up to the ticket counter and asked for the quickest flight to Detroit. If he could get his phone to work, he could book a rental car there, as he'd need to drive from the city to Ann Arbor.

As he waited for the clerk to put in the information and see what flights were available, it felt like he'd never get to his mother. His sister said she'd call or text with updates, but his phone was strangely silent.

"Is there no service here?" he asked the woman at the counter.

"It's the storm," she said. "I'm having a hard time bringing up the flights too." She frowned at her screen and Fisher copied her, the bars at the top of his phone blipping in and out, in and out.

Great. So he couldn't make a phone call to Stacey even if he wanted to. He couldn't text her. He couldn't see if she'd texted him, if Owen had been able to find her and get the message that Fisher was leaving the island for a few days.

Longer than that, he thought, wondering where it had come from. But if there was anything his mother needed, Fisher would make sure she had it. And if that meant he had to stay in Ann Arbor for a while, then he would.

"Ah, here we go." The woman flashed him a smile but barely met his eyes before focusing on her screen again. "I've got a seven-thirty-five or a nine-fifteen."

"As fast as I can get there," Fisher said. He just hoped he wouldn't be too late.

———

By the time he pulled his rental car—which had taken him an additional forty minutes to secure, thanks to the bad weather in Portland that had prevented him from using his app—into the hospital parking lot in Ann Arbor, Fisher hadn't slept in thirty-two hours. His phone had been chiming, buzzing, and otherwise sending notification after notification to him for the past twenty minutes.

But like a responsible driver, and as someone who hadn't

been back to Michigan in too long, he kept both hands on the wheel until he pulled into a parking space. He wanted to take the time to go through the messages, but he didn't really know what condition his mother was in, and he wanted to get to her as fast as possible.

Everything and everyone else could wait.

He hurried inside, feeling like he'd flown halfway across the world without the assistance of an airplane. "Cindy DuPont?" he asked at the reception desk, sure one of his sisters had sent him which room their mother was in.

Armed with the room number, he bypassed the elevators and took the stairs up to the third floor. The first person he saw was Kyla, the taller of the twins by half an inch. She stood and hit Lily, who nudged Denver, who'd leaned back in his seat and had been taking a nap.

"Fish." Kyla hurried toward him and wrapped her arms around him.

"How is she? I'm not too late, am I?"

Lily joined them, and then Denver, a big old DuPont family hug that made Fisher's whole heart squeeze too tight.

"The reception was bad in Portland," he said. "None of your calls or messages came in until about twenty minutes ago."

"She's going to be okay," Denver said. "You're not too late at all. They've got her on heavy medication for her leg, so she's sleeping right now."

Fisher listened to the laundry list of things that his mother was suffering from, the worst of which was a shattered right leg. Other cuts, abrasions, a burn from the air bag, those injuries would heal quick enough.

"What do you guys need?" He cleared his throat and stood. "I'm in desperate need of caffeine. I'll bring back whatever you guys want."

Denver stood too, his brown hair going more and more gray with every passing year. "Let's all go down to the cafeteria. Your mom won't be awake for at least another hour."

Fisher cast a glance at the doors that needed a code to enter, wondering if he really had time to eat. What if she woke up and no one was there?

"It's all right, son," Denver said, putting his hand on Fisher's shoulder. "Let's go eat, and we'll come right back here. Then I'll take you in to see her."

Fisher had felt his fair share of loneliness over the years, especially moving across the ocean to open Sweet Breeze by himself. His mother had been so proud of him, even sending him the article about his swimming pools from *Travel, the Magazine* as if he hadn't seen it online.

But as he stepped into the elevator with Kyla, Lily, and Denver, he felt like he was part of a family again, even if he hadn't been home in a while.

An hour later, Fisher entered his mother's hospital room with tentative steps, hoping she was awake. The nurse who had brought him in went about her business, checking monitors and making notes on a clipboard.

"Mom." Fisher's voice almost broke, but he managed to keep it steady. His mother sat up halfway in bed, her right leg suspended in air, already cast.

"Fisher." Her voice sounded like half-frog, but she put a smile on her face that contrasted with the pain in her eyes. "It's so good to see you."

He approached and bent down to give her a gentle hug. "It took forever, but I made it."

"You can just leave your hotel?"

Fisher took the only chair in the room, glad Denver had offered him the chance to come in alone for a few minutes. "I have plenty of people to run the hotel." He gave her a smile, but his energy was quickly running out. "I'm glad to see you awake."

"Oh, I'm fine." She tried to wave her arm, but it was hooked to an IV and she didn't quite pull it off.

Fisher could tell with one look that his mother wasn't fine. She was always the last one to go to the doctor, and if she got sick, the whole house shut down. Of course, she'd been taking vitamins and supplements his whole life, and she rarely got sick. Seeing her in the hospital bed, with all the beeping and flashing lights, really made Fisher's heart squeeze too tight.

"How long will you be here?" he asked.

"I don't know," she admitted. "The doctor said he'll be back tomorrow to check my leg and then I'll probably have to get up and try walking." She pointed at her broken leg. "Or hobbling. Whatever."

"Denver looks like he agrees with retirement." Fisher leaned back in his chair but kept a close eye on his mom. She looked a lot older than he remembered and when she closed her eyes, she seemed peaceful.

"He's spent a lot of time in the garden," she said, her voice almost a whisper. "What about you? How long will you be here?"

"As long as you need me, Mom."

ALOHA HIDEAWAY INN   197

"Oh, Kyla and Lily are here."

"Kyla and Lily have husbands and families." Fisher shrugged and looked to the slim window. Kyla had been married for three years, and she had a year-old daughter. Lily had gotten married two years ago, and that was the last time Fisher had been home to Michigan. She and her husband didn't have any children yet, but Fisher knew it was difficult to work full-time and maintain a relationship. Just because there was a ring already involved didn't make it easier.

"Denver is an excellent nurse," his mom said.

"You'll find I can make tea and coffee, and order almost anything to be delivered." Fisher pasted a cool smile on his face. "I'd like to stay for a couple of weeks, if you'll have me. I can stay at a hotel, of course."

His mom's house wasn't very big, and she'd converted his bedroom into a yoga studio a decade ago. When she didn't argue, Fisher realized how tired she was.

He was about to stand and go when she said, "So are you seeing anyone in Hawaii?"

A glow moved through Fisher, and he couldn't quite keep his voice even when he said, "You know what? I am. I just started dating a woman named Stacey about a month ago."

"Stacey." His mom smiled. "She sounds nice."

"She has red hair."

"That's great." His mother opened her eyes. "Do you like her? It sounds like you like her."

"I do like her, Mom."

"Why didn't she come with you?"

"I left really quickly," he said. "Dad called and it was during a fireworks show and she was off dealing with a problem at her bed and breakfast." He wanted to check his phone and see if she'd called or texted, but his phone had died during lunch in the cafeteria.

His fingers twitched with need to get to a power source and connect a call with Stacey. He needed to hear her voice. Only she could soothe this ache in his soul, and as he sat in this nondescript hospital room, he realized he might be in love with Stacey.

Might be.

Maybe.

Could be.

"We'll come visit in October," he said. "I was planning to come then, remember?"

"What about the holidays?"

Fisher didn't want to commit. A lot of people went tropical for the holidays, and their first Christmas at Sweet Breeze had been a huge hit. He'd put a massive, twenty-five-foot tree in the lobby and hired an event planner specifically to plan activities for families, children, and couples centered around the holiday.

"She owns a B&B," he said. "And with me and Sweet Breeze, I just don't know if we can make the holidays work." He watched his mom's face fall as she started to nod. "But I'll talk to Stacey. Who knows? Maybe we'll come."

He stood and gave her a quick kiss on the forehead. "I'll send in Denver and the girls for a few minutes. Then we'll let you rest."

"Thank you, Fisher," she said. "You're a good man, and Stacey's lucky to have you."

Fisher grinned and ducked out of the room, thinking his mom had it backward. He was lucky to have Stacey in his life, and he couldn't wait any longer to talk to her. He said he'd be back in the morning, and he hurried out to his rental car. It had no way to plug in his phone, so he drove to the hotel he could see just down the road and got a room.

"How long will you be with us?" the receptionist asked, tucking her dark hair behind her ear.

"I don't know," Fisher said. "Can I just keep the room and let you know?"

"We'll need to charge you for the first night now."

Fisher pulled out his wallet and handed over his credit card. "No problem."

Fifteen minutes later, he finally made it into the room, pausing to take a look around. It was too dark and too cramped though he was sure it was the same size as his rooms at Sweet Breeze. But whoever had chosen the carpet, wallpaper, and curtains had been obsessed with browns and heavy fabrics.

Stop judging. He moved all the way into the room and plugged in his charger, attaching it to his phone. Another minute passed while he waited for it to power on, each second making his blood feel like someone had poured hot chili sauce in it.

He finally got a call to go through to Stacey, his anticipation skyrocketing now. But she didn't answer. Her cute voice came on with, "Aloha. Leave me a message and I'll get back to you."

"Stacey, it's Fisher." He exhaled. He didn't really have anything to say. He just wanted her to tell him about her bed and breakfast, the white chocolate popcorn, and anything else. "Give me a call back when you get this, okay?"

He'd never seen her without her phone in her hand, and the fact that she didn't answer made his stomach feel like someone had dug a hole in the bottom of it.

At the risk of coming off stalkerish, he called her again. The call went to voicemail again. Fisher didn't leave another message.

A series of beeps and chimes came through again, and Fisher looked at his phone, the monumental task of going through all the messages and calls he'd missed over-whelming and exhausting.

He did a quick inventory to see if any of the communica-tions were from Stacey, and found one call and three texts.

Where did you go?

Can you call me please? You're really freaking me out.

I can't believe you left in the middle of the night without saying ANYTHING. At least my first fiancé had the courtesy of leaving me a note.

With every text he read, Fisher's heart beat faster and faster. She thought he'd left her—ghosted her—the way Randy had.

His earlier exhaustion dried up. He didn't care how he came across this time. He called Stacey again, muttering, "Pick up. Please pick up. Come on, Stacey. Pick up."

NINETEEN

STACEY WOULD NOT LET Fisher's absence on the island dictate her behavior. She went about her business of working with Marge in the gardens, cleaning up the beach from the previous night's festivities, and even volunteering to run to the grocery store when Betty needed another fifty pounds of potatoes.

She normally would've sent another employee and headed down the beach to meet Esther and the other women from the Beach Club. But her heart felt two seconds from shattering, and she wasn't sure she could face her friends.

Because Fisher had left the fireworks and her private beach party with all the guests from Aloha Hideaway without a single word. No text. No phone call. No note. Heck, she'd have taken a freaking message he'd stomped in the sand.

She hadn't quite gotten up the nerve to tell Esther about it yet, as his departure was only twelve hours old.

But she did have the fortitude to go to the blasted grocery store, thank you very much. He would not break her the way Randy and then Malik had. He was just a man. A man with a lot of money—and who Stacey suspected now owned a piece of her heart as well. But she'd survived with holes in her most vital organ before. She could figure out how to do it again.

Foolishness more than anything accompanied her through the produce section of the store. She couldn't believe she'd opened herself up to this kind of hurt again. She must be a glutton for punishment or a really bad judge of men. Or both.

Probably both, she thought as she heaved a bag of potatoes into her cart. She repeated the motion a few times and turned to go. The sooner she could get back to her bed and breakfast, the sooner she could hide away in her suite for a few hours. At least until the Beach Clubbers would have to go back home, to work, or simply somewhere else.

Her phone chimed and she practically clawed her purse open to check it. Her heart beat out Fisher's name in an irrational beat, and she hated that. *Fish-er. Fish-fish-er* it cried anyway.

It wasn't Fisher, but Esther. *You're not coming today?*

Busy at the Hideaway. Stacey stuffed the phone away, angrier and more depressed than she had been ten seconds ago. She really hated that a text from the wrong person could do that.

Her phone went off again, but she didn't take it out to look at it. She knew what Esther would ask. *Busy doing what?*

Stacey certainly didn't attend every meeting of the Beach

Club but in all honesty, most of them. If she didn't, there was a big reason why, and everyone knew it. She had a big reason this time, but she didn't want to say what it was.

So she joined the line to check out, keeping her eyes straight ahead as she did. A familiar voice tickled her ear drums, and she told herself not to turn. Not to look.

But she couldn't help herself.

That laugh....

Malik stood several paces away, his dark-haired head tipped back as he laughed at something someone said. A woman stood beside him, and his hand drifted to the small of her back.

Stacey gasped as if he'd touched her there—like he had so many times while they'd been dating and then engaged.

The other woman was Hawaiian too, and her hair had been knotted into an elegant up-do on top of her head. She wore a pure white flower over her left ear, a signal that she was married or in a relationship.

Of course she was. Stacey had heard that Malik and his other fiancée had gotten married. The woman shifted, and Stacey's eyes widened. Not only that, but her baby bump proved that he could make a commitment to a woman and a family.

Just not Stacey. He didn't want her, or to build a family with her.

Tears burst behind her eyes, making them hot and itchy. She couldn't stand here for another second. Not when Fisher wasn't on the island to erase this pain. Not when faced with everything that should've been hers years ago.

Her stomach twisted and cramped, and she snatched her

purse from the cart and headed for the exit. Someone else could come get the potatoes, because Stacey would not be leaving her property for a good long while.

———

That evening, she looked at herself in the mirror. It was obvious she'd been crying for hours. No amount of makeup would be able to cover it up, so she sent a text to Dillan, her night cook, that she would not be able to make it to dinner.

Everything okay? Dillan's text made Stacey weepy again, but she pushed against the tears. If she let them take over, she'd spiral into the chest-aching sobs she'd already endured that afternoon.

Just not feeling well. Stacey sent the text and checked for other messages, even going so far as to power down her phone and restart it. Surely Fisher wouldn't just *leave her* without saying *anything*.

Would he?

She'd thought he was different than other men. She scoffed as the phone stayed stubbornly notification-less. "Yeah, he has a lot of money. That makes him different all right."

She'd already sent him a text that morning, asking him where he'd gone. He hadn't answered it. Whether he'd read it or not, she couldn't tell. Desperate, and grasping at something to help rid her of seeing Malik with his pregnant wife, she tapped out another message for Fisher.

Can you call me please? You're really freaking me out.

Maybe he was hurt. Or ill. Or somewhere where there was absolutely no cell reception. Maybe his phone had died.

As her brain sifted through the thoughts, she realized she was making excuses for him. She wanted him to respond, call, knock on her door and sweep her into his strong arms.

Her phone remained silent, and no one rapped at her suite. She shivered, cold despite the tropical heat that kept everything just a little too warm in July, and let the tears come again.

By the next morning, Stacey wasn't as sad as she was angry. Esther had called twice the night before, and Stacey felt like she could face her friend today. Besides, she needed her help.

"Hey," Esther said. "You fell off the face of the Earth yesterday. What's up?"

"Have you seen Fisher at all?"

"Why would I see Fisher?"

"Well, you drive a lot of guests to and from Sweet Breeze, right?"

"Yeah." Esther drew the word out dangerously. "But it's not like Fisher's the valet."

He probably just hadn't gotten to that part of the under-cover work yet. Stacey sighed. "I need your help tracking a credit card number."

Silence came through the line, and Stacey pressed her eyes closed, hoping Esther wouldn't say no. Her father was some sort of financial securities guy, and she could ask him to look into such things from time to time.

"Whose credit card number?" she finally asked.

"Well, I don't exactly have the number. Just a name."

"Who?" Esther pressed, practically barking the word.

"Fisher," Stacey said. "He disappeared during the fireworks on the Fourth. I want to know if he's left the island, and he'd use his credit card to do that." At least she hoped he would. She'd never seen him pay with cash when they went out—always a card. "He has an American Express he likes."

Esther let out a long hiss. "He left? He didn't say anything to you?"

While Stacey didn't want to repeat the story, Esther deserved it. And she'd tell her eventually anyway. So she told the tale of the locked door and how she'd been gone for maybe twenty-five minutes only to return to the beach and find him completely gone.

"I haven't heard from him since."

"Maybe he's hurt."

"I've been through all of that," Stacey said. "I just want to see if he used his credit card for a flight or something."

If he'd left the island, Stacey didn't know what she'd do. She'd been telling herself all these weeks that the third time was the charm. That Fisher would not take her heart and abandon her the way Randy had. That he would never cross the channels and find a new, more exciting girlfriend.

"Let me call my father," Esther said. "Give me a few minutes."

"Take your time," Stacey said. After all, Fisher had been AWOL for almost thirty-six hours. What was another one where she didn't know?

It only took Esther half an hour to call her back and say,

"He left on the twelve-twenty-four flight to Portland, July fifth."

Stacey felt like the air had been punched out of her lungs. "Thanks, Esther." Her voice hardly sounded like her own. She held the phone away from her ear and looked at it like she had no idea how to use the device.

Esther's voice could be heard, but Stacey ended the call before the sob working its way from her core to her throat could be recorded.

Didn't matter. Esther showed up at Aloha Hideaway ten minutes later, looking tan and windswept and more concerned than Stacey had ever seen her. She carried two fruity drinks, one in each hand, and a bag containing take-out.

"Shrimp spring rolls," she said. "And all the noodles Leolai would let me take." She set the food on the table in the corner of Stacey's suite. She hadn't moved from the bed, and Esther surveyed her.

"Did you shower today?"

Stacey shook her head, numb. "I saw Malik at the grocery store yesterday." Her chin wobbled and she took a tight breath to stop herself from crying. "His wife was pregnant."

Esther swooped toward Stacey and said, "Oh, honey."

Stacey let her gather her into her arms and she cried into Esther's shoulders. "I'm never going to get married and have a family." When she'd started thinking she'd have a houseful of boys with Fisher's dark hair and blazing blue eyes, she wasn't sure. Only that she had, and it hurt so, so much that he'd left the island without even texting her.

Hours later, Stacey's tears had dried up and her sadness

had oscillated back and forth between despair and pure fury. At the moment, she was so angry she couldn't even enjoy her hibiscus flowers. And that made her even angrier.

She wanted to talk to Fisher so badly it made her teeth grind together. She didn't dare dial his number, actually afraid that he might answer and she might start yelling. Or sobbing. Or blubbering about the pregnancy of another woman that she so desperately wanted to be hers.

And she hadn't even spoken with Fisher about a family, children, what to do with her dogs and cat, nothing. And there was some stupid little speck of hope in the back of her mind that told her not to ruin everything quite yet. That maybe if they got back together, she didn't want him to think of her as the crazy redhead who called and screamed from an ocean away.

So she texted him instead. *I can't believe you left in the middle of the night without saying ANYTHING. At least my first fiancé had the courtesy of leaving me a note.*

She read over the words once, twice, three times. Then she sent them. Fisher had more resources than a piece of paper and a pencil, and she let her phone drop to her lap. Why hadn't he said anything? Sent someone over to tell her? Surely he had people who could do that.

Something swirled through her thoughts, and she seized onto a tiny corner of one of them. Fumbling the phone now, she couldn't dial Sweet Breeze fast enough. And they answered too fast for her to order her questions.

So she just blurted out, "Fisher DuPont."

"Mister DuPont isn't in today," the man said. "Is there a message I can leave for him?"

"Who's second in charge?" she asked. Fisher had mentioned the name of his general manager several times, but Stacey had never met the man.

"That would be Owen Church."

"I'd like to speak to him then."

"One moment please." The line started playing low, classical music, the kind that drove Stacey bananas. It took Owen several long minutes, wherein Stacey almost lost her nerve and hung up, before Owen came on the line.

"This is Owen Church," he said.

"Owen," she said, practically shouting his name. "It's Stacey Stapleton from Aloha Hideaway?" Why she phrased it as a question, she wasn't sure.

"Yes, Stacey. What can I do for you?"

Stacey inhaled deliberately. "I'm just wondering where Fisher is."

"Fisher?"

"Yes, your boss? Owner of the hotel where you work? Fisher DuPont?" She couldn't quite keep the bite out of her voice.

"I'm sorry," he said. "I'm confused. Didn't you get the message I sent over to Aloha Hideaway yesterday morning?"

Stacey blinked, the furniture across her bedroom going out of focus. Blink, blinked. "No," she said.

"I sent it quite early. Perhaps you didn't have anyone at the desk." He spoke with a dignified gentleness that suggested to Stacey that he was trying to be tactful but also communicate to her that he'd sent the message.

"I don't know," Stacey said. "But I never got it. Would

you—?" She cleared her throat. "Would you mind telling me what the message said?"

"Of course," Owen said. "I got a phone call from Fisher near midnight on the Fourth. He didn't come back to the hotel, but said he had to go home. He asked me to keep things going here, keep him updated on anything I needed to via email or text, and to let you know he'd call you as soon as possible."

Stacey's heart soared, but quickly came back to the ground with a skidding crash. "Home? Why did he need to go home?"

"His mother was in a car accident." Something scuffled on the other end of the line, and Owen said, not to her, "Yes, just one moment."

"I'll let you go," she said, her earlier foolishness roaring through her now with the strength of river rapids. She hung up before she could start crying again.

But this time the tears weren't because of a broken heart. She dialed Esther and said, "I need you to come over and help me plan a trip."

"You're taking a trip? Where?"

"Michigan," Stacey said. "As soon as possible."

TWENTY

FISHER ONLY SLEPT because he couldn't physically stay awake any longer. His body had limits, and he'd passed them long before checking into the hotel. So when he woke, his phone lay on his chest, right where it had fallen when he'd nodded off.

Stacey had not called. Or texted.

Owen had though. No voice mail. No texts. Just a missed call from a couple of hours ago. He dialed his general manager, though he really couldn't do anything about rowdy tourists from half a world away.

On the fourth ring, Owen answered with, "Fisher, I'm sorry I can't talk right now. I'm on the phone with Cooper. Zach's having an attack."

Concern spiked in Fisher's pulse. Owen's younger son suffered from asthma and panic, and one triggered the other. "No problem. Call me later."

Owen ended the call, and Fisher stood up, pushing out a

long sigh. Did he dare try Stacey again? Why hadn't she gotten his messages and called him?

He wasn't sure, but he felt like he'd been sweating for hours, and then been rolled in dirt. So he chose the shower, hoping the hot water would make him feel more human again. Help his thoughts get in the right order. Put together the pieces of the puzzle that was Stacey Stapleton and come out the other side with a more complete picture.

Nothing quite gelled, and he had another message when he stepped out of the steamy bathroom. "Fisher," Denver's voice said on the voice mail. "Mom's awake, and Kyla made her famous cinnamon rolls if you want to come over."

"Is she home?" Fisher wondered aloud before he realized he was listening to a message. His brain wasn't working properly and whether that was from the jet lag, the time difference, or the lack of sleep, he wasn't sure.

What he knew was that he needed to talk to Stacey before this ache in his head would subside. So he tried calling her again, something about her radio silence not adding up. When she didn't answer, Fisher's frustration reached a level he hadn't allowed himself to get to since working with his biological father.

He called Denver, vowing that if he didn't answer, Fisher might just chuck his phone out the window. But his stepfather did answer, and Fisher asked, "Mom's home already?"

"She made great progress, and the doc said she could go home. You know your mother. She didn't want anyone fussing over her longer than necessary."

Fisher did know that about his mother. "I'm on my way, then."

"Can you stop and get a couple of things?"

"Of course."

Denver gave him a short list of treats his mother particularly loved, and Fisher confirmed that he'd get them all. He went through the motions of checking for his wallet and the keys to the rental car. But he was prolonging the moment he left the hotel, for a reason he couldn't name.

He eventually went out to the car and got behind the wheel. He realized that he didn't feel fit to be around people, especially when his problems seemed so small in comparison with the health challenges his mother was facing.

But he did like cinnamon rolls, and he did want to take his mother the ginger ale and dill pickle chips that she loved. Denver said they'd already bought the movies she wanted as digital downloads, and that her reading device was fully charged.

As Fisher pushed a cart aimlessly around the grocery store, he thought about his life and if this would be all he had for the rest of it. He'd been fulfilled and busy with the design, build, and opening of Sweet Breeze. He loved his hotel. But it didn't fill the same hole in his soul that Stacey had.

You don't love her, he told himself as he picked up more chips than anyone needed to have. He added a box of the butteriest microwave popcorn he could find, wishing he could recreate the movie theater stuff.

He felt dangerously close to falling in love, like he'd

climbed to the top of the highest volcano in Hawaii and had all ten toes on the edge of the pinnacle.

He'd just pulled up to his childhood home when his phone rang. His heart leapt to the back of his throat and bobbed around there for a few seconds, the insane hope that it would be Stacey on the other end of the line.

But it was Owen, and Fisher was concerned about Zach, so he answered. "Hey, Owen. How's your son?"

"He's resting now, thank you."

Always so formal. Fisher wanted to remind him that they were friends, but he didn't have the energy this time. "I was returning your call earlier. You didn't leave a message."

"Oh, right. Miss Stapleton called and apparently, she never got the message that you'd left the island to tend to your mother."

Horror felt like icy needles in his veins. "No wonder she won't answer my calls."

"I'm sorry, sir. I sent the message first thing in the morning. I don't know what happened."

She thought he'd ghosted her. Left her without a word. And worse, she was right. He *had* left her private party in the middle of a show without saying anything. The panic he'd felt had been so real, so consuming, he'd only acted on instinct. And everything inside him needed to get to Michigan.

"It's fine," he heard himself say, but he wondered if Stacey would ever talk to him again. She'd told him about her two failed engagements, and Fisher didn't have immediate plans to ask her to marry him. But the more time they spent together, the more he'd thought about it. Still, he wasn't oblivious to the things they still needed to talk about: their living situations, children, their expectations, the prenuptial agreement....

He pressed his eyes closed and said, "Tell me about Zach."

"Sir?"

"How is he? You sounded flustered when I called."

"I...was. But he's calmed now."

"Did you have to use the thunder jacket?"

"Yes." Owen's voice was barely above a whisper.

"Did it help?"

"Immensely." Owen cleared his throat. "Thank you." Whether he meant for the jacket or for asking, Fisher wasn't sure. He didn't care. When he'd learned that Owen's son suffered from panic attacks, he'd done some research and bought the boy a thunder jacket, similar to what they used to soothe anxious dogs.

"I'm glad it helped." Fisher looked toward the house as Lily came out the front door. She leaned her hip into the railing at the top of the steps and folded her arms. "I have to go. Don't worry about Stacey."

Fisher ended the call and went to see what his half-sister wanted. He collected the groceries from the back seat of the rental car and approached her. "What's going on?"

"Oh, you know. Mom being Mom. And you taking over an hour to stop for a handful of groceries."

Fisher climbed the steps and handed her one of the bags. "I'm...distracted."

"Obviously. What's her name?"

"Stacey."

Lily's eyebrows went up. "Oh, so you're not even denying it."

"Why would I deny it?" Fisher gazed down at her evenly, trying to figure out what he'd missed.

"You're…different than when you'd left."

"I should hope so."

She ran her finger along the very pressed edge of his collar. "So polished. Sophisticated."

A lot of money would do that to a man, but Fisher kept his mouth shut. His family knew what he'd done in Hawaii. Surely Lily knew he had money.

She turned and went in the house. "Come on, then. Mom's been dying for those chips."

Fisher endured the visit, only for his mother's sake. But he wanted to get back in the car and make the tortuous trip back to Hawaii. If Stacey wouldn't answer her phone, he'd go to her. Explain everything. Make her understand. Kiss her and tell her he would never leave her the way the other men in her life had.

As the afternoon wore on, Fisher's energy waned, and he wanted nothing more than to return to his hotel and figure out how to get in touch with Stacey.

He eventually left and went back to his dingy room. He called Stacey, but she didn't answer. Angry now, he called Marshall.

"Have you talked to Esther or anything?"

"About what, exactly?"

"Stacey."

"Why would I talk to her about Stacey?"

"Apparently she thinks I left her."

"Did you?"

Fisher pushed his breath out. "My mother was in a car accident. I'm in Michigan. Temporarily."

"But you did leave without telling her." Marshall wasn't asking.

"I asked Owen to send her a message, and she never got it."

"Esther said she's not in a good place. Maybe give her some time."

"Yeah." Fisher didn't want to give Stacey time. He had no idea how long he'd be in Michigan, but he couldn't stand the thought of not being able to call her at night, tell her what had happened that day, be assured that she'd be there for him when he returned.

With nothing else to do, and no one to call, he settled on the bed and switched on the TV. He woke to the sound of knocking on his door, and he blinked open his eyes. Darkness bathed the room, and Fisher didn't know how much time had gone by. Hours, at least.

The knocking came again, this time more insistently. No one identified themselves, and his stomach growled as he approached. He peered through the tiny peephole in the door, and then his fingers couldn't get the locks unlatched fast enough.

"Stacey," he said, not sure he believed the redheaded goddess standing in the hall outside his room was real.

She wore her nervousness right on her face, in those beautiful eyes. "Can we talk?"

Fisher swept her into his arms and inhaled the scent of

her skin. He caught the sweetness of pineapple, along with the saltiness of the sea he loved so much.

"I'm so glad you came," he whispered. He pulled back and bent down as if he'd kiss her.

She stiffened and said, "Not until we talk."

TWENTY-ONE

STACEY WANTED to be swept away with Fisher, and she had a hard time being in the same room with him and not kissing him. But her fingers wound around each other, just like they'd been doing for the hours and hours it had taken her to get here.

"It's a long way from Getaway Bay to Ann Arbor." She forced a laugh out of her lips, hoping Fisher would accept her apology. Accept *her*.

"Yes, it is."

"How's your mom?"

Fisher tilted his head and looked at her, the dim light in the hotel room between them. "So you got my message? Why didn't you call?"

Stacey paced away from him, toward the window covered with awful drapes. "I didn't get it until…." She pushed her breath out and faced him. "I thought you'd left me in the middle of the night. I spent a lot of time crying and then I went to the store to buy potatoes and I saw Malik."

Fisher's fists balled and his eyes tightened. But he didn't speak, and Stacey didn't know what she wanted him to say anyway.

"His wife is pregnant." Stacey turned back toward the window, wishing she hadn't jumped to so many conclusions, wishing her heart wasn't still so weak, wishing she'd have picked up her phone when Fisher had called.

If only life were made of wishes, and that they always came true.

"Do you want children, Stacey?" Fisher's voice entered her ears softly, almost as a caress.

She nodded. "Yes."

"I do, too." His words wrapped themselves around her like a warm blanket.

"I'm getting older," she said. "And seeing him, with her, it hit me really hard. It...that was supposed to be my life." She lifted her chin. "And I felt like it had been stolen from me once, and then twice, and you were gone, and I'm not even really sure when I started thinking we could maybe get married." She swallowed, almost choking on the word.

"Or have kids, but all the thoughts were there once you weren't." A tear splashed onto her cheek, and she swiped it away as quickly as it had come.

"I did leave suddenly," he said. "I'm sorry about that. I asked Owen to notify you."

Stacey nodded, her emotions quaking inside her. "I know."

Fisher took a step toward her. "I wouldn't just leave you without saying anything."

"I know that. I do." She looked away from him, but her eyes came right back. "I'm sorry I jumped to that conclusion. I really like—" Her throat closed, and she pulled in a deep breath. "I love you, and I should've known better." The room swam, and Stacey couldn't believe she'd said she loved Fisher.

A smile burst onto Fisher's face. "Stacey." Her name, those two syllables, conjured up so much between them. "I love you, too."

Relief poured through Stacey as if someone was filling her from top to bottom with hot water. "You do?"

Fisher approached slowly, as if she were a squirrel he was trying to entice to stay. "I do." His hands cupped her face, and Stacey leaned into the hot touch, her eyes drifting closed.

"I'm not quite whole," she whispered. "I know that now, but I know I can be. *Will* be." She opened her eyes and looked right into Fisher's ocean-blue ones.

"I can wait."

And those three words became the best Stacey had ever heard. "Yeah?"

"Of course. We still have a lot to talk about and decide. But we'll do it together." He brushed her hair back and leaned closer. "Okay?"

She nodded, a rush of gratitude and relief and love consuming her. "Okay." She tipped up on her toes. "I think I'm ready for that kiss now."

His lips twitched into a half smile. "Oh yeah?" He slid

one hand behind her back and brought her closer. Stacey closed her eyes and it seemed to take him ages to bring his mouth to hers.

But when he did, he kissed her in that slow, sensual way of his that made her blood warm one degree at a time until she was scorching hot. She felt the usual tenderness in his touch, but something hotter too, like desire. Something gentler, like love. And Stacey had learned that it took both in a relationship for it to truly succeed.

She pulled back slightly and whispered, "I love you," one more time, just to make it all the way real.

————

"Do you think they'll like me?" Stacey smoothed down her blouse, wishing she'd had time to iron it. Fisher lounged in the armchair near the window in her hotel room, barely glancing at her.

"Of course they'll like you." He finished whatever he was doing on his phone and stood. "My mom likes everyone."

"I haven't met anyone's family in a really long time." She hated the way her blood felt like it had frozen and someone was cracking it. "Of course, I haven't done a lot of things in a while."

"Better get used to it, I suppose," he said. "Lots of changes coming."

Stacey tried not to think about it, but she'd been up all night stewing over the things they'd talked about. Everything from where they'd live after they got married to the items they'd both want in their pre-nuptial agreements.

Stacey had thought she'd be resistant to signing one, like it would signal that Fisher didn't trust her. But as he spoke in that rhythmic, sexy voice of his, she realized she had plenty of assets that needed protecting. When she'd asked if he'd sign an agreement with her, he hadn't batted a single eyelash.

"Of course," he said. "It's a good idea for us to both have one."

She'd stayed in his arms until the wee hours of the morning, and then she'd gone down the hall to her own room. Their discussion hadn't been the only thing keeping sleep from her. The idea of staying with him, sleeping with him, also took up a lot of brain power. But it was different than the time she'd tried to seduce him during the storm.

That would've been just sex.

But if they went to bed together now, Stacey was terrified she'd give so much of herself to him that she'd never recover if something went wrong.

Nothing's going to go wrong, she told herself. Fisher wouldn't sleep with her anyway, something else they'd talked about. He wanted to wait until the wedding, and Stacey had readily agreed. She found something alluring about the idea of having his complete devotion before she gave him everything of herself.

She'd mentioned eloping, and he was considering it. "I'm simply worried my mom won't like that," he'd said. She understood that, and maybe wearing his diamond ring wouldn't yield the same results as her previous two attempts.

"Stace?" His hand landed on her arm, startling her out of her thoughts.

She looked up at him. "Yeah?"

"I asked if you were ready. We're going to be late."

She looked back at her reflection again, giving the blouse up for a lost cause. "I'm ready."

He brushed his lips along the soft skin below her ear. "They're going to love you," he whispered. "Just like I do."

She grinned and turned into his arms. "Let's go then."

Her nerves took the form of butterflies as they drove from the hotel to his parents' house, following her all the way up the front steps. The yard was meticulously kept, with bright green grass that had been mowed recently. The flowerbeds were weed-free and filled with beautiful blooms.

Fisher opened the door and called, "Mom?" but an older gentleman turned from the bar in the kitchen which sat at the back of the house.

"Fisher." He bustled forward saying, "Your mom's asleep. She had a rough night and needed a nap already."

A frown pulled Fisher's eyebrows down, but he swept it away quickly. "All right. Something still smells great." He tucked Stacey into his side. "Denver, this is my girlfriend, Stacey. Stacey, my step-dad, Denver."

"Nice to meet you." Stacey smiled and shook the man's hand. He had a kind spirit and bright eyes that had a smile of their own.

"And you." Denver looked back and forth between her and Fisher. "Come on in. She made that French toast casserole you like so much." He bustled around the kitchen, getting out syrup and powdered sugar. He opened the oven and pulled out a bubbling pan full of cinnamon coated bread cubes.

"I can see why you like this," Stacey said.

"Oh yeah?"

"Yeah." She bumped him with her hip. "You have an unhealthy obsession with cinnamon."

Fisher chuckled. "Maybe. But we all have our obsessions." He flashed Stacey a private look that said something about the fruity drinks she loved.

She joined him at the bar and gladly accepted a big scoop of the French toast casserole. She didn't think she'd be able to eat, but since Fisher's mother wasn't around, Stacey managed to get a few bites down. She wasn't sure why, but she really wanted to impress his mom. He spoke so highly of her, and he'd dropped everything on the island to come be here with her.

At the first sound from down the hall, Fisher leapt from his barstool and said, "I'll go check on her."

Stacey watched him disappear down the hall, then heard his low voice speaking before he came out again, this time behind a woman with his blazing blue eyes. She hobbled on a pair of crutches, with Fisher's hands hovering behind her just in case she stumbled or fell.

"Stacey." His mother spoke in such a bright tone it rivaled the sun. "Oh, Fisher, she's beautiful. Way out of your league."

Fisher smiled and shook his head. "I know, Mom."

Stacey laughed uncomfortably. "It's so nice to meet you, Cindy. Fisher talks about you non-stop."

"Oh, Fisher doesn't do anything non-stop except work."

Cindy gave a little laugh and let him help her settle at the dining room table.

"Hey," he said. "I haven't been working for a few days now."

Stacey decided not to mention that he'd been on his phone all morning. "I get it," she said. "I run my own bed and breakfast, and it is constant work."

"Come, sit." Cindy patted the table in front of the seat beside her. "Tell me all about Hawaii. Fisher says it's wonderful."

Stacey beamed at him and then her before moving to sit down. "It is wonderful. The flowers are beautiful, and my grandfather cultivated a unique color of hibiscus I grow in my gardens. You'll have to come visit to see them."

"How did you know I love gardening?" she asked. "Is Fisher telling all my secrets?" She laughed, and Stacey joined in, more relaxed than she'd thought she'd be. She'd imagined Fisher's parents to be imposing and sophisticated the way he was. But they were down-to-earth people who baked breakfast and planted bulbs.

And Stacey loved them, just like she loved Fisher's pressed slacks and clean-cut look. Just like she loved Fisher.

TWENTY-TWO

FISHER HATED WAVING to Stacey as she moved through the security line at the Detroit airport. But she wore a big smile and a short pair of shorts, turning away from him when it was her turn to present her ID and ticket.

He turned around too, wishing he was going back to Hawaii with her. She'd stayed for a few days, but she didn't have general managers and dozens of team leads to keep Aloha Hideaway running. She also didn't have unlimited funds for a hotel room, though Fisher had offered to pay.

One of the things they'd talked about was that he wouldn't pay for things until they were married. Well, she'd allow dinner and her fruity drinks, but he wouldn't pay for new carpet in her bed and breakfast until after the nuptials.

Too bad she'd show up to brand new carpet when she returned to Aloha Hideaway. He couldn't help himself, and he wanted Stacey to know that he didn't really care about spending his money on her. He certainly had enough of it, and if he couldn't spend it on who and what he wanted, what was the point?

Instead of going straight back to the house, Fisher stopped off at a jeweler he'd spent nights researching after Stacey had left his hotel room. He couldn't believe he'd fallen in love with her so fast, but it felt freeing to say it to her. Kiss her without holding back his feelings. Shop for diamond rings without consulting her.

Stacey loved a good surprise, and Fisher was determined to give one to her in the form of a proposal. And since he wasn't returning to Hawaii for another ten days, he had plenty of time to figure everything out.

Ten days. It sounded like a lifetime to Fisher, but the first couple of hours were eased by the glint of diamonds and the prospect of marrying the woman he loved.

———

The moment his plane touched down on the runway, the air changed. Fisher had decided he didn't hate it, nor did he hate the squeal of a certain redhead as he came out of the airport. Stacey threw her arms around him and laughed, and Fisher's heart swelled and beat faster.

No matter what the old adages said, in his case, absence did not make the heart grow fonder. He wanted to hold Stacey every day, breathe in the floral scent of her hair, and kiss her. Every day.

"I missed you." She giggled and pulled back, glancing at him. "Do you always travel in a three thousand dollar suit?"

"Not always." He picked up his briefcase with one hand

and laced his free fingers through hers. "Today, I happen to have a meeting."

"I thought we were going to lunch."

"We are. The meeting is right after that." Fisher ran his hand through his hair and glanced down at Stacey. Now that he was here, face to face with her, concealing his engagement plans was going to be harder than he thought.

His phone buzzed, and he waited until Stacey slid into the black town car before checking it. Esther. He definitely didn't want Stacey to see her best friend's name on his screen. But he'd needed someone close to Stacey in his back pocket to take care of some of the finer details of his little escapade.

All set, her text read. He still wasn't sure what was going on with her and Marshall, as his best friend had remained quite mute on the topic. Fisher had been so preoccupied with other things, but he'd be talking to Marshall soon enough.

Rather than responding, Fisher slipped his phone into his pocket as he ducked into the car. Stacey started into easy conversation about everything he'd missed on the island while he'd been in Michigan, and before he knew it, the car arrived at the beachside taco stand that sold fresh fish the owner caught in the morning and sold until it was gone. Sometimes he opened for dinner, and sometimes he didn't.

Today, the line for his catch of the day ran several people deep, but Fisher didn't mind the wait. After all, he didn't really have a meeting to get to, and Stacey had never asked for specifics so he didn't have to lie.

He took a deep breath of the tropical, ocean air and

exhaled loudly. "Wow, I missed life here." It felt slower, more normal, filled with less expectations. Which was strange, because his entire life—his whole fortune—was here, hinged on the success or failure of Sweet Breeze.

"My mother is still planning on us for dinner," Stacey said.

"Right. Dinner with your parents." He'd seen them before, but he'd not met them the night they stayed in his hotel. "Looking forward to it."

"Really?" She squeezed his hand. "Doesn't sound like it."

He chuckled and set aside his nerves. They didn't belong to dinner with her parents anyway. Maybe he was rushing into this engagement. Maybe he should just keep things in the serious dating category for a while.

But that didn't sit right in his gut either. He'd never wanted to rush into anything with Juliana or any of his previous girlfriends, no matter how serious they'd gotten. But this relationship with Stacey felt like it filled the void in his life so completely that he couldn't do without it.

So he stepped up to the counter to order his mahi-mahi fish tacos, warmth now radiating through him. That could've been the hot July sun, or the sand baking beneath his feet. But Fisher hoped it was the love he had for Stacey that had him sweating.

They ate their tacos in the shade, the breeze from the bay tugging at his hair and the silence between them comfortable.

He made a big show of checking his phone and stretching his legs before standing. "Time for my meeting."

"Already?" Stacey squinted up at him.

"Where are your sunglasses?" he asked. She loved her mirrored lenses, and he rarely saw her outside without them.

"Oh, I lost them a couple of days ago and haven't gotten a new pair yet."

He extended his hand for her to take. She did and he pulled her up. "Well, let's go get you some."

"Right now?"

"I think we have time before my meeting."

Their car was waiting right where it had dropped them off, and Fisher checked to make sure Esther was behind the wheel now. The switch was supposed to happen while he and Stacey ate fish tacos, right on schedule.

He couldn't tell, because the driver kept their face turned away, and a small smile touched his lips. Of course Stacey would recognize her best friend and Esther wouldn't want that. He hoped this hadn't been too hard for her, but he didn't really know her that well personally. He knew she ran a tight business, was never late, and always acted professionally. Whatever Marshall had done, he better fix it.

Once they were settled in the back seat, the car eased forward and took them toward Sweet Breeze. Fisher hadn't told Stacey where his meeting was, but his hotel made sense. Sure enough, she didn't question it.

Getting her out of the car and up to the fifteenth floor would be much more difficult, but thankfully Fisher didn't have to be the one to do that. He kissed her and got out of the car as if he'd leave her in it to go back to Aloha Hideaway until dinner with her parents that night.

He went straight up to the fifteenth floor using the

regular guest elevator, his heart thumping irregularly in his chest. He had Owen, Marshall, Esther, and Tayla in on the plan, and Stacey should be arriving in fifteen minutes or less. Depending on how many questions she asked and how difficult she was, he could possibly have a normal pulse again soon.

The room looked exactly as he'd described to Owen and Marshall, with a few dozen of her garden's purple hibiscus flowers in beautiful vases—one on the table, one in the window, and one on the armoire holding the television.

The black ring box he'd overnighted to Marshall a few days ago sat on the table too, and Fisher picked it up and cracked the lid. He hoped Stacey would like the princess cut and the traditional yellow gold. Hoped she'd say yes.

He replaced the ring on the table and slicked his hands down his thighs, almost desperate for this event to be over so he could release this anxiety.

His phone buzzed and he checked it quickly. Owen had said, *She's on her way up with Esther.*

Fisher took a deep breath and held it for a few seconds. Esther had not detailed how she'd get Stacey up to the fifteenth floor. There were no pools, no amenities, nothing. Just guest rooms. But Esther had said she'd take care of it, and Fisher had left it at that. Perhaps Esther had simply told Stacey what Fisher's plans were. He hoped not, as he'd made it clear to everyone that he wanted this to be a surprise.

He couldn't hear voices in the hall. He'd made sure his hotel had the best sound-proofing in the business, after all. A few more minutes passed, and he wondered how long it took for a couple of women to come up fifteen floors in the best elevator money could buy.

Finally the door beeped and it cracked a bit, and Fisher leapt for the ring box.

"You've been staying here since Saturday?" Stacey's voice came through the break in the door.

"Yes. And I just need another set of eyes to find the earrings." Esther's tone was perfection; she was playing this part amazingly well.

"The seashell ones. Got it."

The door opened, and Stacey entered. She stopped short when her eyes met Fisher's. "What—?" She scanned the hibiscus before her eyes came back to Fisher standing there in his *five* thousand dollar suit, holding that ring box.

"Fisher?"

"Stacey," he said, making his voice as even as possible. It still trembled slightly. "I'm in love with you, and I don't want to wait to make you my wife. I know it's fast, but sometimes when two people fall in love, it happens quickly."

He dropped to one knee and cracked the lid of the ring box. "Will you marry me?"

Her hand fluttered around her neck before pressing against her heartbeat. "Fisher." She spoke in a warning tone, like he was joking or something.

Fisher waited, his question asked. And he certainly wasn't joking. She took a step forward, but only when Esther nudged her. "Go on," Esther hissed.

"Are you serious?"

"I'm not down on one knee for fun." Fisher rarely knelt

before anyone. His confidence wavered for one, two terrifying breaths before she rushed him.

Dropping to the floor she took his hand holding the ring box in both of hers. She snapped the lid closed after looking at the diamond for only a moment. "Yes." She laughed, tears streaming down her face.

"Yeah?" Fisher asked, just to make sure.

Stacey nodded, smiling and crying and trembling. "Yeah."

He grinned too, his own nerves finally settling into stasis. "I love you." He bent forward and kissed her. "I want you to be mine." He leaned his forehead against hers, enjoying the way she cradled his face in her hands, claiming him.

"I love you, too, Fisher."

And with those words, he opened the box again and slipped the ring on his fiancée's finger.

———

Read on for a sneak peek of **GETAWAY BAY**. You'll get to see what's going on with Esther and Marshall!

SNEAK PEEK! GETAWAY BAY CHAPTER ONE

ESTHER PINNETT GROANED as she rolled over and silenced her alarm. At least it wasn't dark despite the earliness of the hour. She should be used to getting up by five o'clock, but it still seemed like a chore every morning.

She sat up, the tropical breeze coming through the open window only a hint of the storm that was coming toward the island. Sighing, she got herself into the shower, choosing to use her purple shampoo that morning, along with a blonditioner that was supposed to make her highlights brighter.

So she'd been coloring her hair for a few years. It was still naturally blonde, but every once in a while, everyone needed a bit of help. Esther took hers in the form of coffee with caramel and cream, and hair dye. It wasn't a crime.

She brushed her teeth, put magnesium oil on her softer upper arms, and went through her hair routine with the creams and gels and dusts.

Esther thrived on routine. Lived for it. Stepped into her

neatly pressed black slacks and paired them with a blue, white, and black flowery blouse, exactly the same way she did every morning. Just before she left her bungalow for the day, she'd put on her black suit jacket, all she ever wore on the island, rain or shine.

True, she didn't drive every day, but her first client of the morning did sometimes work seven days a week. And it was seven days a week of torture, because her first client of the day was Marshall Robison.

Tall Marshall, with dark-haired, black sand-colored eyes, and the richest man in the islands. And the man Esther had had a secret crush on for two years.

Two very long years.

Over seven hundred days of torture, driving him from his cliff-side mansion to his offices at the Robison Plantation, the largest conglomerate of pineapple plantations in the islands. Sometimes she drove him to the beach. Or to his favorite restaurants. Or to his best friend's hotel, Sweet Breeze, right on Getaway Bay.

He also went to multiple company functions, each with a different woman on his arm. Esther had started giving those jobs to someone else, as she could hardly stand to be in the car with him and his giggly girlfriend-for-the-night.

She knew how he took his coffee, that he did a crossword puzzle every single day, and that his birthday was coming up in just a couple of days. She also knew she wanted more than one date with the man who didn't go on second dates. She wasn't sure what that made her, other than delusional.

Hopeful, she told herself. *Optimistic*.

After she'd brushed her teeth, slipped into heels, and applied her makeup—in that order—she went into her airy kitchen. Bending to smell the fresh flowers she kept on her small table for two, Esther took three seconds from her routine to take a deep breath and face another week. Marshall had texted her business number last night to confirm he needed a ride this Sunday morning, and that meant a long work week.

With the storm, though, Esther had already canceled all the jobs for Tuesday and until noon on Wednesday. Even the afternoon clients knew that it might not be safe to drive around the island after the storm. It was just too unpredictable, though Esther had never seen the weather shut down the island for very long.

Even if she wasn't driving that morning, she didn't make her own coffee. So she put her credit card and her driver's license—which she kept in a slim billfold—in her front right pocket, and a tube of mint Chapstick in her left. After shrugging into her jacket, she plucked the keys to the sleek, black Lincoln town car from the hook by the carport door and went outside.

The scent of sea and flowers met her nose, and she took another moment to savor it. She wasn't a Hawaii native, but she did enjoy living here.

She got behind the wheel and headed for The Roast down the street. Sunday didn't normally see too many people before six a.m., so there was no wait. Victoria leaned out of the window, her face brightening when Esther rolled down her window.

"Esther. Aloha. The usual?"

"Plus one," she said, which was her code to get her coffee as well as one for Marshall.

Vic knew how to make them, and she ducked back into the hut. Several minutes later, Esther lifted her to-go cup to her lips, the sweet caramel and the rich cream making the dark roast coffee delicious.

A sigh passed through her whole body and she twisted to accept the second cup.

Marshall's coffee. Regular roast. One splash of chocolate. One of milk. He took his richness in the cocoa, not the cream, and Esther had tried his concoction once, on a morning when he didn't need a ride. Vic hadn't been any the wiser, because Esther had gotten her usual too.

And while she thought nearly everything Marshall did was perfect, she much preferred her caramel cream concoction to his.

Not that it mattered. Marshall barely knew her name, and if he had to pick her out of line-up, Esther felt sure that he'd fail. Even the women he took to fancy dinners and business parties barely got a glance from him.

She handed over the cash for the coffees and eased the car back onto the road. It was a twenty minute drive up twisty, turny roads to Marshall's cliffside mansion. Esther could make the drive in her sleep, and sometimes she did. She never wore her power suits in those fantasies, but fun, flowy, flowery dresses, with flirty footwear and lip gloss the color of ripe raspberries.

Her hair flowed over her shoulders, and Marshall pushed it back to kiss her bare skin there.

She cleared her throat and her thoughts, and glanced at

herself in the rear-view mirror. Maybe she seemed a bit flushed, but that could've been from the coffee, or the humidity. She completed the drive and parked with the front bumper right up at the gate.

Marshall never buzzed her in; she'd never seen the inside of his home. He came down the black, asphalt driveway, always wearing a perfectly tailored suit in black, gray, or navy blue. Esther much preferred the navy ones, and as he approached today, Esther didn't deviate from her routine.

She got five seconds to ogle him, and then she'd look straight through the windshield, acknowledge him professionally, and unlock the doors.

Today her five seconds saw him saunter toward her, so sexy and so untouchable it hurt. When her time was up, she turned and looked at her birthday gift for him on the back seat. Should she grab it now before he saw? What would he think?

She'd been driving him for years and never given him a birthday present. He'd never acted like it was his birthday on the day of, but he'd mentioned his summer birthdate a few years ago. Esther was a master at remembering small details. Her knack for it had kept customers loyal to her for long periods of time, and she trained all her drivers to pay attention to what people told them as they drove around the island.

She gave him a single nod and clicked the locks open. Marshall always sat on the passenger side, in the back seat. Today was no different. His long legs came first, followed by that toned body that must see hours in a gym.

Esther wrenched her thoughts from his body and

watched as he spotted the blue-wrapped package on the seat.

"What's this?" He lifted it, the pale paper contrasting with his half-dark skin.

"Happy birthday, sir," Esther said.

He shook his head and started to chuckle. "You never cease to amaze me. How do you remember all that you do?"

"Oh, I can't reveal my secrets." She could also never reveal how warm his words made her.

"Should I open it?"

"Sure, go ahead."

He ripped the paper along the tape, always so proper. She wondered what it would be like to see him in a pair of shorts, casually eating with friends, or spending time with his family. She knew the Robison's were a tight-knit group, as she drove him to his parents' home every Thursday for dinner.

There really was so much to learn about a person just by watching them.

His laughter filled the car, and it was glorious. Esther wanted to bottle it and unstop it in the few moments before she fell asleep at night, so it could accompany her into sleep.

"A crossword puzzle book." He held it up for her to see, as if she didn't know what she'd wrapped. "Thank you, Esther." He gazed at the book with fondness, and when those dark eyes switched to her, he lit up her whole world.

She cleared her throat again and adjusted her sunglasses to make sure she wasn't giving anything away. That was another thing about Esther. She could hold an incredible amount of information and emotion close to the vest.

"Of course, sir," she said, flipping the car into reverse. She watched him covertly, and he flipped through the pages of the puzzle book, appreciation in his eyes. He glanced up at her a couple of times, but Esther kept both hands on the wheel and her eyes forward.

Marshall liked music, but nothing too loud. So the tropical tunes played at level three, and Esther's heart beat seemed to be bumping in time with them. Down, down, down she drove, and Marshall seemed to be watching her more than usual, which means he didn't immediately bury himself in his phone or something from his briefcase.

But he kept stroking his thumb along the cover of the puzzle book and looking at her. It was so out of his routine that by the time Esther pulled up to the pineapple plantation, she was positively jumpy. She managed to keep her hands still on the wheel though she felt like squirming and twitching.

Marshall also didn't heave a sigh and get out the way he normally did. He leaned forward like he might say something to her, but in the end, he settled back against the seat.

"Thank you again," he said, his voice like the hibiscus honey she loved in her evening tea. Warm, sweet, thick.

"Happy birthday," she said. "I hope the storm doesn't ruin it."

A smile lit up his face and he collected his coffee and his briefcase, and he got out of the car, the way he always did. He walked toward the steps, the same way he had yesterday and every day before that.

But then he paused, turned around, and looked at her.

Seemingly right at her, despite the mirrored lenses and layers of glass between them.

Esther pulled in a breath and then pulled away from the curb, cursing herself for buying the man a birthday gift. She may as well have screamed, "I have a crush on you!" and left it at that.

———

Get your copy of GETAWAY BAY now and go with Esther and Marshall as they find their island happily-ever-after.

BOOKS IN THE GETAWAY BAY RESORT ROMANCE SERIES

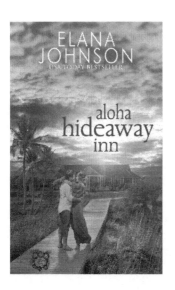

Aloha Hideaway Inn (Book 1): Can Stacey and the Aloha Hideaway Inn survive strange summer weather, the arrival of the new resort, *and* the start of a special relationship?

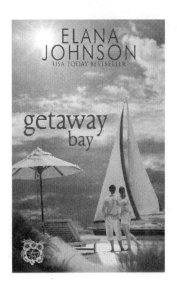

Getaway Bay (Book 2): Can Esther deal with dozens of business tasks, unhappy tourists, *and* the twists and turns in her new relationship?

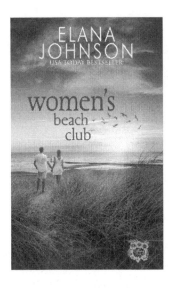

Women's Beach Club (Book 3):
With the help of her friends in
the Beach Club, can Tawny solve
the mystery, stay safe, and keep
her man?

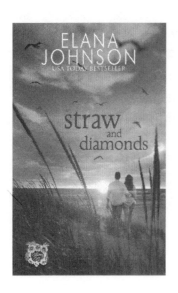

Straw and Diamonds (Book 4): Can Sasha maintain her sanity amidst their busy schedules, her issues with men like Jasper, and her desires to take her business to the next level?

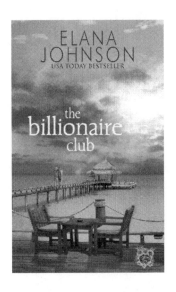

The Billionaire Club (Book 5): Can Lexie keep her business affairs in the shadows while she brings her relationship out of them? Or will she have to confess everything to her new friends...and Jason?

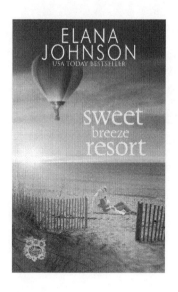

Sweet Breeze Resort (Book 6): Can Gina manage her business across the sea and finish the remodel at Sweet Breeze, all while developing a meaningful relationship with Owen and his sons?

Rainforest Retreat (Book 7): As their paths continue to cross and Lawrence and Maizee spend more and more time together, will he find in her a retreat from all the family pressure? Can Maizee manage her relationship with her boss, or will she once again put her heart—and her job—on the line?

Getaway Bay Singles (Book 8):
Can Katie bring him into her life, her daughter's life, and manage her business while he manages the app? Or will everything fall apart for a second time?

Turn the page to view series starters from a couple of my other series!

BOOKS IN THE GETAWAY BAY ROMANCE SERIES

Escape to Getaway Bay and meet your new best friends as these women navigate their careers, their love lives, and their own dreams and desires. Each heartwarming love story shows the power of women in their own lives and the lives of their friends.

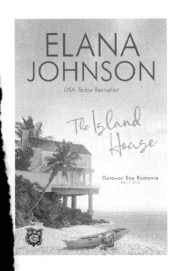

The Island House (Book 1): Charlotte Madsen's whole world came crashing down six months ago with the words, "I met someone else."

Can Charlotte navigate the healing process to find love again?

BOOKS IN THE STRANDED IN GETAWAY BAY ROMANCE SERIES

Meet the McLaughlin Sisters in Getaway Bay as they encounter disaster after disaster...including the men they get stranded with. From ex-boyfriends to cowboys to football stars, these sisters can bring any man to his knees when the cards are stacked against them.

The Perfect Storm (Book 1): A freak storm has her sliding down the mountain...right into the arms of her ex. As Eden and Holden spend time out in the wilds of Hawaii trying to survive, their old flame is rekindled. But with secrets and old feelings in the way, will Holden be able to take all the broken pieces of his life and put them back together in a way that makes sense? Or will he lose his heart and the reputation of his company because of a single landslide?

BOOKS IN THE HAWTHORNE HARBOR ROMANCE SERIES

Escape to the beach today with single moms, single dads, and that one old lady that knows everyone in town... This sweet and clean romance series is sure to have the heartfelt love stories and heartwarming women's fiction you're looking for.

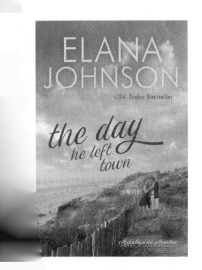

The Day He Left Town (Book 1): He's waiting for a promotion to come through. She's back in her hometown after a humiliating break-up. Can Tony and Cat make their second chance stick this time?

ABOUT ELANA

Elana Johnson is the USA Today bestselling and Kindle All-star author of dozens of clean and wholesome contemporary romance novels. She lives in Utah, where she mothers two fur babies, works with her husband full-time, and eats a lot of veggies while writing. Find her on her website at feelgoodfictionbooks.com

Made in the USA
Las Vegas, NV
16 August 2024

93895129R00159